LAST WILL

(legal thriller)

Alex Kane

Nathan felt a knot in his stomach. The elderly billionaire Joseph Langley knew he was dying. He didn't care much about that—death was inevitable. He was more concerned about what he would leave behind. Specifically, who he would leave it to.

His six children had been waiting for years for him to finally die so they could pounce on his fortune. They were all equally spoiled, greedy, and incapable of managing the wealth he had spent decades building. So he made a decision that would shake their world.

A few hours before his death, he signed a new will.

*****

Nathan Bishop had never liked probate. He worked at a midsize Washington law firm, doing divorces, real estate, and the occasional small lawsuit. He was no legal star—and he didn't want to be.

That's why he was surprised when one morning his boss called him into his office and announced:

— You will represent the heir of Joseph Langley.

Nathan raised his eyebrows.

— Which one?

— None of them.

Nathan frowned.

- Meaning?

The boss passed him an envelope.

— Langley's will is different than anyone expected. His entire estate, almost two billion dollars, was left to a woman no one has ever heard of .

Nathan opened the envelope. There was only one name inside.

Rachel Price.

— Who is she?

The boss shook his head.

— We have no idea.

A few days later, Nathan found Rachel Price. She lived in a small town in Montana, worked as an English teacher, and, most importantly, had no idea who Joseph Langley was .

"This must be some mistake," she said as they sat down in her modest living room.

"That's not a mistake. The records are clear. Joseph Langley left his entire estate to you."

— But why?

— I was hoping you would tell me that.

Rachel shook her head.

— I've never heard of this man.

Nathan saw sincerity in her eyes. She wasn't faking it. And yet the will was unequivocal.

"His children have already hired lawyers," he said. "They intend to contest the will."

Rachel looked at him worriedly.

- What does it mean?

"That means unless we can prove Langley had reason to sign his fortune over to you, they can take it all back."

— But I don't even know who he was!

Nathan nodded.

— That means we have to find out.

*****

Two days later, someone broke into Rachel's house.

They didn't steal anything valuable. They didn't take any money or jewelry. But all of her family photos—albums, flash drives, old letters— were gone.

When Nathan arrived, Rachel was distraught.

"Is this a coincidence?" she asked.

Nathan shook his head.

— There are no coincidences.

He had a bad feeling about this.

If Joseph Langley left two billion dollars to a woman who didn't know he existed, it meant one thing: he was hiding a secret someone didn't want revealed.

*****

Nathan didn't like to work in the dark. He liked facts, documents, testimony. But everything in this case was a mystery – from Langley's will to Rachel Price's life. If they were to win in court, they had to find proof of why the billionaire had left her everything.

He started with what was the simplest: Rachel's birth certificate.

He filed a request for a copy at the Montana Vital Records Office. When he received the document, something immediately caught his eye.

Father: **unknown.**

Mother: Eleanor Price.

Rachel sat in his office and stared at the document.

— My mother never spoke about my father. I asked her as a child, but she always avoided the subject.

Nathan looked at her carefully.

—Is it possible that Langley was your father?

Rachel shook her head.

— That's absurd. I never met him. Besides, my mother had no connections with rich people. She worked as a nurse.

Nathan thought for a moment.

— And if he wasn't your father, then maybe... someone else?

Rachel shrugged.

- I have no idea.

But Nathan did.

If Joseph Langley knew Rachel's mother and left his entire estate to her daughter, it meant that something had happened in the past that was supposed to remain a secret.

And someone really didn't want them to know about it.

*****

That evening Nathan returned to his apartment and saw that the door was slightly ajar.

He stopped.

His heart started beating faster.

He slowly took out his phone and dialed the police number, but before he could press "call," he heard a low, calm voice from inside the apartment:

— Don't do that.

Nathan froze.

- Who are you?

— Come in and close the door.

Nathan stepped inside cautiously. In the chair across from his desk sat a man in a dark suit. About fifty, gray hair, a tired face.

"Who let you in here?" Nathan asked, trying to sound confident.

— Don't worry. I didn't come to threaten you.

— So what for?

The man leaned back in his chair.

— To get you to drop this matter.

Nathan burst out laughing.

— Of course. What else?

The man took an envelope from his inside pocket and placed it on the desk.

— Two million dollars.

Nathan looked at her in disbelief.

— Are you kidding?

— Absolutely not.

— And if I refuse?

The man sighed.

— Then they'll stop making you offers and start making threats.

Nathan looked at him carefully.

— Who sent you?

— People who have more to lose than you think.

Nathan was silent for a moment.

— You know what's funny?

- What?

—That you just made me want to do it even more.

The man sighed, got up from his chair and walked to the door.

"You're not stupid, Bishop. But I don't think you know what you're getting yourself into."

Nathan watched him leave.

When the door closed, he sat down heavily in the chair.

Two million dollars for your silence.

This meant one thing: the truth is worth much more.

*****

The next day, Nathan flew to New York. If he wanted answers, he had to start with the one person who knew Joseph Langley better than anyone else—his attorney and confidante, Richard Thorne.

When he entered his office on the fiftieth floor of a luxury skyscraper, his secretary looked at him with a cold smile.

— Mr. Thorne does not receive unannounced visitors.

"I'm not unannounced," Nathan said, handing her his business card. "I'm Rachel Price's lawyer."

The secretary turned pale.

She stared at the paper for a moment, then nodded.

— Please wait.

A few minutes later, the door to the office opened. Nathan walked in and saw a tall, elegant man in his sixties sitting behind a huge mahogany desk.

"Mr. Bishop," said Richard Thorne quietly. "I was expecting you."

Nathan sat down across from him.

— I have a few questions about Joseph Langley's will.

— It is valid and legal. There is nothing to discuss here.

— This remains to be seen.

Thorne sighed.

— You shouldn't be here.

- Why?

Thorne looked at him carefully.

— Because some people will do anything to ensure that this case never goes to court.

Nathan smiled slightly.

— That's funny. That's exactly what the guy who tried to bribe me with two million dollars told me.

Thorne didn't move, but Nathan saw his jaw clench.

There was silence for a moment.

Finally Thorne leaned over the desk and said quietly:

"If you really want to know why Joseph Langley left his entire estate to Rachel Price... you should start with her mother."

Nathan frowned.

—Eleanor Price?

Thorne nodded.

— Yes. And you should hurry.

Nathan narrowed his eyes.

- Why?

Thorne leaned even closer.

— Because if you don't do this, it may soon be too late.

Nathan left Richard Thorne's office with even more questions than he had before. Who was Eleanor Price? Why had Langley given his entire fortune to her daughter? And why was someone willing to pay two million dollars to keep this case from ever going to trial?

He had to start from scratch. Rachel's mother could be the key to everything.

He returned to Montana and met Rachel at her house.

— Your mother. Tell me everything you remember about her.

Rachel shrugged.

— She was a wonderful person. Warm, caring, and worked as a nurse at the local hospital. We never had much money, but I never felt like I was lacking anything.

— What about her past? Where did she come from?

Rachel thought for a moment.

"I know she was born on the East Coast, Virginia I think. She moved to Montana when she was young. She never told me why."

— And your father?

— She never talked about him.

Nathan made a mental note of this.

— What if it wasn't a random decision? Maybe she was running away from something... or someone?

Rachel looked at him worriedly.

"Do you think this has anything to do with Langley's will?"

- I'm sure.

Nathan pulled out his phone and searched state public records for Eleanor Price's birth certificate. Within minutes, he found what he was looking for.

Born: **May 18, 1952, Richmond, Virginia.**

But that wasn't the most important thing.

Maiden name: **Eleanor Langley**.

He looked at Rachel.

"Your mother... was the daughter of Joseph Langley."

Rachel looked at him in stunned silence.

— It's impossible.

Nathan handed her the phone.

"Eleanor Price is Eleanor Langley. Daughter of Joseph Langley. Your mother was his only biological child."

Rachel shook her head.

— But why didn't she ever tell me about it?

Nathan thought for a moment.

— Maybe she cut off contact with her family? Maybe she was cursed?

Rachel still looked stunned.

"And if that's true... then the will makes sense. Langley left his estate to me because I was his only real granddaughter."

Nathan nodded.

— Yes. And that means his adopted children—the ones now fighting over the inheritance—have no rights to his fortune.

Rachel looked thoughtful.

"If my mother was Langley's daughter, why didn't he ever try to contact me?"

Nathan already had his suspicions.

— Maybe... someone made sure you never met.

*****

That same evening, Nathan received a call from a private investigator he had hired to check Eleanor Price's background.

"I have something you might be interested in," the detective said. "But not over the phone. We have to meet."

- Where?

— Hotel Regal, room 417.

Nathan knew the hotel – it was on the outskirts of town, discreet, and rarely visited by tourists. It was the perfect place for conversations that didn't want to be overheard.

When he arrived, the door to the room was ajar.

He felt a familiar tightening in his stomach.

He slowly walked inside.

There was silence in the room.

The detective was lying on the bed. Dead.

There was a piece of paper on the floor next to his hand.

Nathan lifted it carefully.

"Don't ask any more questions."

Nathan went back to his office and locked the door. He knew that this wasn't just a matter of the will anymore. Someone was killing people to keep the truth from coming out.

He looked through Langley's files. He found information that in the 1970s, Joseph Langley had been at odds with his own father, who ran a law firm and political deals with people who were better left unspoken.

Then something else occurred to him.

Langley hasn't just had one enemy in the past. He's had many.

He began searching through the newspaper archives. After a few minutes, he found an article from forty years ago.

The headline was:

"Tragic accident on the East Coast. Car of tycoon Joseph Langley's daughter plunges off cliff. Body never recovered."

Nathan stared at the screen.

The body was not found.

Eleanor Langley survived. She went into hiding. She changed her name, disappeared, and started a new life as Eleanor Price.

And now someone wanted the truth to never come to light.

Nathan returned to Rachel.

— Your mother… ran away from someone.

Rachel stared at him with wide eyes.

— Do you think someone tried to kill her?

Nathan took a deep breath.

— Yes. And I think that someone is still out there.

Rachel felt herself go cold.

— So what now?

Nathan looked at her seriously.

"Now we need to find proof that Langley knew your mother was alive. Because if we do that, no one will be able to contest the will."

Rachel swallowed hard.

— What if that someone still wants to silence us?

Nathan reached for the phone.

— Then we will be ready.

But deep down he knew they weren't.

Because if someone has been hiding this secret for forty years… they won't stop now.

Nathan had been up all night, going through documents, reports, old newspaper articles. He had to find proof that Joseph Langley knew his daughter had survived. If he could, the will would be unchallenged—and Rachel would inherit the entire fortune.

But if he was wrong…

Then they'll face the best lawyers in the country in court, and his opponents will do everything they can to bury the case. Maybe literally.

In the morning his telephone rang.

"Nathan?" Rachel's voice was nervous. "You have to come here."

- What happened?

— Someone was in my house.

Rachel stood on the porch of her small home in Montana, wrapped in a warm sweater, holding a mug of half-finished tea. She was pale.

"They didn't steal anything," she said as Nathan walked in. "But… someone was here."

The house looked the same as always, but Nathan noticed details. Kitchen drawers were slightly ajar. Photo albums had been taken off the shelves. Someone had left a book open on the desk.

This was no ordinary burglar.

This was someone who was looking for something.

"Are you missing something?" Nathan asked.

Rachel shook her head.

- I don't know.

Nathan looked at the albums.

— Photos of your mother. Do you think they were looking for something in them?

Rachel frowned.

- I don't understand.

Nathan picked up one of the albums and began to leaf through the pages. Photos of Rachel as a child, her mother, snapshots of vacations, holidays, birthdays. Then he stopped at one photo.

Rachel was sitting on the beach, maybe five years old. Eleanor was standing next to her, smiling, wearing a straw hat.

Behind them, in the background, there was a man.

Nathan squinted. The man was standing in the distance, but something about his figure looked familiar.

— Rachel, do you know who this is?

Rachel looked at the photo.

- I have no idea.

— Do you have more photos from this trip?

Rachel went to the bedroom and returned a moment later with an envelope.

Nathan flipped through the photos. In one shot, Eleanor was walking along a wooden walkway. Behind her, in the shadows, stood the same man.

Nathan reached for his phone and took a picture of the photo.

— I have to check it out.

Nathan sent the photo to an FBI analyst friend. Within an hour, he had a response.

— Nathan, where did you get this photo?

- Why are you asking?

—Because that man is Martin Caldwell.

Nathan frowned.

— Should I know him?

"Maybe not. But Joseph Langley certainly knew him. He was his personal bodyguard for thirty years."

Nathan froze.

— Security guard?

— Yes. And then suddenly he disappeared.

- When?

— In 1984. Right around the time Eleanor Langley "died" in the accident.

Nathan felt a shiver run down his spine.

"So you're telling me that Joseph Langley's bodyguard, who should have been dead forty years, appears in photos with Rachel and her mother when she was a child?"

— It looks that way.

Nathan looked at Rachel, who was listening to the conversation.

"What does that mean?" she asked quietly.

Nathan took a deep breath.

— That means your mother didn't escape on her own. Someone helped her.

Nathan now had two new questions.

First, if Martin Caldwell hid Eleanor for years, where is she now?

Second: who was trying to find them – and why?

Rachel opened another album and began looking through the photos.

— I remember my mother had an old friend. I don't know who he was, but he would come to our house sometimes, they would talk for a long time, and then he would disappear for months.

Nathan looked at her carefully.

— Do you have his name?

Rachel thought about it.

—His name was... Henry Blackwell.

Nathan quickly typed the name into the database. The results came up immediately.

Henry Blackwell, former lawyer of Joseph Langley.

Nathan swore under his breath.

—Your mother ran away, and her only contact was someone who worked for your grandfather.

Rachel turned pale.

— Do you think she trusted him?

Nathan shook his head.

— I don't know. But if anyone has the answers, it's him.

Nathan and Rachel found Henry Blackwell in a small house in North Carolina. He was old, gray, and had the look of a man who had carried heavy secrets for too long.

"You shouldn't be here," he said as he opened the door.

"We have no choice," Nathan said.

Blackwell looked at Rachel and said nothing for a long moment.

"You're her daughter," he finally whispered.

Rachel held her breath.

— Did you know my mother?

Blackwell nodded.

— I helped her escape.

— From whom?

Blackwell looked at them seriously.

— From her own father.

Nathan blinked.

— Before Langley? He left her daughter his entire fortune!

Blackwell shook his head.

—Because he had a guilty conscience. But then, forty years ago, he wanted Eleanor gone.

Rachel took a step back.

- Why?

Blackwell hesitated, then said quietly:

— Because she knew something about him she shouldn't have.

— What's this?

Blackwell took a deep breath.

—Your grandfather didn't make his fortune legally. He had dealings with people he didn't want to know. And your mother... found out the truth.

Nathan swallowed.

— And that's why he faked her death?

Blackwell nodded.

— Yes. And now the people who helped him back then still don't want you to find out the truth.

Nathan looked at Rachel.

— What now?

Blackwell responded without hesitation.

"If you want to survive... you have to find Martin Caldwell before they do."

*****

Nathan had never been one to chase ghosts, and Martin Caldwell was just that. A man who should have been dead for forty years suddenly becomes a key piece of the puzzle.

"Do you know where he is?" he asked Blackwell.

The old man looked at them hesitantly.

— He had been living in Costa Rica for the past twenty years. He had a small house there, and he led a quiet life.

— And now?

Blackwell sighed.

— The last time I spoke to him was a month ago. He said he felt like someone was watching him.

— Do you have his number?

Blackwell rose from his chair and pulled out an old address book. After a moment, he found what he was looking for.

"Here's his contact," he said, writing the number down on a piece of paper.

Nathan picked up the phone and dialed the number. It rang three times.

On the fourth call, someone picked up.

"Hello?" The voice was low, tired, cautious.

— Mr. Caldwell?

Silence.

— Who are you?

— My name is Nathan Bishop. I'm Rachel Price's attorney.

—Rachel...?

— Eleanor's daughters.

There was a long silence on the other end.

And then he heard the whispers.

— I'm being watched. I can't talk on the phone. If you really want to know the truth, you have to come to Costa Rica.

Nathan looked at Rachel.

- When?

— Tomorrow. And don't fly under your own name.

The connection was lost.

Nathan put the phone down.

Rachel stared at him with wide eyes.

— Are we going to Costa Rica now?

— It looks like so.

Nathan didn't like trips into the unknown. Especially ones that could end with a bullet in the back. But two days later, he and Rachel got off at the small airport in San José, rented a car, and headed for the coast.

Caldwell lived in an isolated house on the edge of the jungle, a few miles from a small fishing village. They arrived late in the afternoon.

The house was made of wood, modest, with a wide terrace overlooking the ocean.

Rachel knocked on the door.

There was no answer.

Nathan tried again.

Nothing.

They looked at each other.

"Maybe he left," Rachel said.

But Nathan felt something was wrong.

He pushed the door open. It was open.

They entered carefully.

The house was empty.

But there was an open laptop on the table in the living room. Next to it was a phone, still connected to the charger.

And on the floor…

"Oh God," Rachel whispered.

There was a dark stain of blood on the wooden boards.

Nathan quickly looked around the house.

— They may have taken him, but he's still alive.

Rachel glanced at her laptop. A text editor window was open on the screen.

Nathan sat down and began to read.

"If you're reading this, it means I didn't get to tell you the truth. You need to find the documents I hid. Langley's real will. The real reason Eleanor had to disappear. Look where it all began. In Richmond."

"Richmond…" Rachel whispered. "That's where my mother was born."

Nathan looked at her.

—That means we have to go back to Virginia.

But before they could get out, they heard the sound of an engine.

Nathan looked out the window.

Two black SUVs were approaching them down the road.

"We have problems," he said quietly.

Nathan grabbed Rachel's hand and pulled her toward the back exit.

— We have to escape.

They ran out the back of the house and headed toward the jungle. They heard the SUV doors slam shut.

"Split up!" came a voice.

Rachel looked at Nathan in horror.

- Who's that?

Nathan had no idea, but he knew one thing: they weren't friends.

They ran through the dense vegetation, weaving between trees until they reached a small path leading down the hill.

Nathan stopped, catching his breath.

"We need to get to the car. If we get to the main road, we could lose them in the city."

— What if they catch us?

Nathan looked into her eyes.

— Then they'll have to try harder.

They sped toward the San José airport, adrenaline pumping through their veins.

"Who was that?" Rachel asked, looking in the mirror.

"The people who have been keeping the truth from coming out for forty years," Nathan replied.

— But why now?

—Because Langley's will be compelled them.

Nathan looked at Rachel.

— The question is: What did your grandfather know that was so important that he was afraid to reveal it until his death?

Rachel swallowed hard.

— We'll find out in Richmond.

Nathan turned into the airport.

If they were to find answers, they had to go back to where it all began.

But deep down he knew one thing.

They weren't the only ones going there…

*****

The flight to Richmond took less than four hours, but Nathan felt as if time had stood still. Sitting next to Rachel, he looked through a stack of documents he had managed to copy from Martin Caldwell's laptop before they had fled his home in Costa Rica.

There were bank account numbers, old transactions, names.

"See anything familiar?" Rachel asked, staring at the screen.

Nathan nodded.

—A few names come up repeatedly. Richard Thorne, Henry Blackwell... and someone with the initials MC

Rachel frowned.

—MC? Martin Caldwell?

Nathan shook his head.

"I thought about that. But there are transfers here from the last five years. Caldwell was in hiding. Someone else was handling those transactions."

— Do you have any suspicions?

Nathan looked at the last line of the document.

—Not yet. But I have a feeling we'll find the answer in Richmond.

It was midnight when they reached the city. Nathan rented a room in a small hotel near the center and immediately fired up his laptop.

"We need to find where Eleanor could have hidden these documents," he said, looking through years-old files.

Rachel sat down next to him.

"Mom said she grew up in a big old house. It might have been Langley's family property."

Nathan quickly checked the land registers.

— Bingo. The Langley Mansion, built in 1912. Last occupied in 1984 ... which was exactly when Eleanor disappeared.

Rachel held her breath.

— Do you think the documents are there?

— This is the only place that makes sense.

— What if someone is already looking for them?

Nathan looked at her seriously.

— That's why we have to be first.

The Langley residence was on the edge of town. When they pulled up to the old gate, they saw that the grounds looked deserted.

"Are we going in?" Rachel asked.

"We didn't come here for a picnic," Nathan said, and opened the gate.

The house was huge, although time had taken its toll. The paint was peeling from the walls, the windows were dusty, and wild bushes were growing around them.

Rachel glanced at the front door.

— Closed.

Nathan walked along the building and found an open window. He climbed up and opened it wide enough for them to enter.

As they stood in the dark hallway, Rachel lowered her voice.

— What now?

Nathan took out a flashlight.

"We're looking for the office. If Langley hid anything, it's there."

They walked cautiously through the house. The smell of old wood and dust filled the air. Eventually they reached a room that must have been a study.

Nathan looked around. A desk, shelves full of books, an old clock on the wall.

— If there's something here, we need to find it fast.

They began searching the room, Nathan checking drawers and Rachel turning books on shelves.

Then they heard a bang.

Rachel looked at Nathan.

— Did you hear that?

Nathan held his breath.

They were not alone.

They turned off the flashlight and hid behind a shelf. A moment later they heard heavy footsteps in the hallway.

Someone entered the office.

Nathan saw a shadow moving in the darkness. Two people.

"Search here," said a low, hoarse voice.

Rachel looked at Nathan with wide eyes.

Nathan pointed to the window on the other side of the room.

They had to get out.

They slowly moved towards the window, but suddenly…

— Someone was here.

Nathan heard someone moving toward them.

There was no time for subtlety.

He grabbed Rachel's hand and rushed to the window.

The glass shattered as they jumped outside. Rachel fell to the grass, and Nathan landed next to her.

— Run!

They headed toward the car. Behind them, they heard shots.

The bullets hit the ground nearby.

Nathan opened the car door and pushed Rachel inside.

— Pedal to the metal!

The engine roared and they took off with a screech of tires.

In the mirror he saw two men standing in the driveway.

They didn't have time to find the documents. But now they knew they were on the right track.

Rachel was still breathing heavily as they drove back into the city.

— Who were they?

Nathan shook his head.

— I don't know. But if they were there, it means the documents are still in the house.

Rachel looked at him in shock.

— Do you want to go back there?

— Not now. But we have to find a way to get there before they do.

Nathan's phone buzzed.

He looked at the screen. Number unknown.

— Hello?

"Mr. Bishop," he heard a familiar, cold voice.

Richard Thorne.

"We need to talk," the lawyer said.

— About what?

—What Joseph Langley was really hiding.

The meeting took place at a fancy restaurant on the outskirts of town. Thorne sat alone at a table, calm, as if the whole situation were routine to him.

"What do you know?" Nathan asked, sitting down across from him.

Thorne smiled slightly.

— I know you won't give up. And I know you're close to the truth.

— And you want me to let it go?

— On the contrary. I want you to meet her.

Nathan raised his eyebrows.

- Why?

Thorne sighed and leaned forward.

"Because the people who kept this secret for years made one mistake. They let Joseph Langley live to an old age. And now, after his death, everything could come out."

— What's this?

Thorne looked him straight in the eye.

— Joseph Langley hid the truth about his family his entire life. But his will wasn't his biggest secret.

— So what?

Thorne smiled slightly.

— Who he was really protecting all these years.

*****

Nathan Bishop wasn't a man who trusted people easily, and Richard Thorne was definitely not trustworthy. He was part of the system. He had served Langley as a lawyer and confidant for years, and now he was suddenly claiming to help.

"I don't believe you," Nathan said, taking a sip of coffee.

Thorne smiled slightly.

— And you are doing good.

— So why are we here?

"Because I know that you and Rachel went back to Richmond, that you were at the old Langley place, and that you were almost shot there.

Nathan was silent.

"These men who attacked you," Thorne continued, "are not acting alone. They are merely executors. Someone sent them."

- Who?

Thorne leaned across the table and looked Nathan in the eye.

—The men who guarded Joseph Langley's secrets for years.

Nathan narrowed his eyes.

— I thought you were his confidant.

Thorne smiled bitterly.

—I was his lawyer. Not the keeper of his secrets.

— So who was he?

Thorne took a deep breath.

"The real power in the Langley family was not Joseph's, but his father and grandfather's. Joseph had tried for years to distance himself from them, but he could never truly do it. He was the heir to an empire they had built on deals, bribery, and—if the old rumors were to be believed—a few bodies buried in unmarked graves."

Nathan looked at him carefully.

— And you were part of all this?

— I was a lawyer. I made sure everything was legal. I didn't ask questions.

— Until now.

Thorne nodded.

— Because Joseph Langley, in the last years of his life, realized something he had refused to see before. That not everything can be hidden.

— What do you mean by that?

Thorne looked at him seriously.

—Joseph Langley spent his entire life hiding someone. Someone who shouldn't be alive.

Nathan felt a knot in his stomach.

—Eleanor.

Thorne nodded.

— Yes. And he didn't do it of his own free will.

Nathan narrowed his eyes.

— What do you mean?

Thorne leaned back in his chair.

"Do you think Langley faked his daughter's death? That he forced her to run away?"

— And not?

Thorne shook his head.

— No. She ran away because she was afraid of her own father.

- Why?

—Because she discovered he wasn't who everyone thought he was.

Nathan was silent for a moment.

— What did she know?

Thorne looked him straight in the eye.

—That Joseph Langley spent years financing an organization that eliminated his enemies.

Nathan stared at Thorne in silence.

"Are you telling me Langley had his own... group of killers?"

"Let's put it more elegantly," Thorne said with a hint of a smile. "He had a 'crisis management agency.'"

— And in practice?

— People who fixed problems before they became scandals.

Rachel, who had been listening in silence until now, finally spoke up.

— My mother knew about this?

Thorne nodded.

— Yes. And that's why she had to disappear.

Rachel swallowed hard.

— My grandfather tried to kill her?

Thorne hesitated.

— I don't know. All I know is that after her "accident" everyone stopped looking for her.

"Except for one man," Nathan said.

Thorne looked at him questioningly.

—Martin Caldwell.

— So you found him after all.

—Not exactly. He found us and then disappeared. Someone got to him before we did.

Thorne sighed.

— That means we're running out of time.

— For what?

Thorne looked at Nathan carefully.

— To discover who's really pulling the strings.

Nathan frowned.

— I thought it was Langley.

"Joseph Langley was not without guilt, but he was trying to redeem himself at the end of his life. He didn't leave Rachel his will by accident. It was his final message. His way of revealing the truth."

— What truth?

Thorne leaned over the table.

— That his family had been part of something much bigger for decades. A web of power and influence that controlled politicians, banks, the courts.

— Conspiracy?

— Let's call it a system. And now the system wants to make sure that no one finds evidence of its existence.

Rachel spoke quietly.

— So the documents we are looking for…

Thorne nodded.

— This is the only proof of how far the tentacles of this organization have reached. And that is why they are willing to kill to get them back.

Nathan took a deep breath.

— Where should we look?

Thorne smiled slightly.

"Return to the Langley residence. You couldn't have stayed there long enough to search the house thoroughly."

— And those people who attacked us?

— They were just puppets. Real players never get their hands dirty.

Nathan looked at Rachel.

— We have to go back.

Rachel swallowed hard but nodded.

- All right.

Thorne leaned on the table.

— If you find documents, you have to release them. You can't keep them to yourself.

"What about you?" Nathan asked.

— My role is over. I have given you everything I know.

Thorne reached for his coat and stood up.

— Good luck, Mr. Bishop.

Nathan watched him leave.

Rachel turned to Nathan.

— Do you think we can trust him?

Nathan looked at her seriously.

— No. But if he wants to deceive us, the best way to find out is to go where he sent us.

Rachel took a deep breath.

— We're returning to the Langley residence.

Nathan nodded.

— Yes. But this time we'll be prepared.

Nathan and Rachel drove in silence through the night streets of Richmond. Their minds were full of questions, but one was paramount: were there really documents in the Langley mansion that could destroy the entire deal?

"This could be a trap," Rachel said, looking out the window.

Nathan tightened his hands on the steering wheel.

- I know.

— So why are we going back there?

"Because if Thorne was telling the truth, this is our last chance to get evidence."

Rachel didn't look convinced.

— What if he wasn't telling the truth?

Nathan looked at her.

— That means someone wants to lure us there.

Rachel took a deep breath.

— And yet we're heading straight into a trap.

"Yes," Nathan said. "But this time we'll be ready."

He took a gun out of his pocket.

Rachel looked at him in disbelief.

— Do you really have a gun?

— I hired a private security guard on the black market in Miami. When he saw what I was getting into, he threw in a free gun.

"Great," Rachel muttered. "Now we'll end up dead for sure."

— Not if we do it quickly and quietly.

As they turned onto the long, winding road leading to the mansion, Nathan turned off his lights and slowed down.

"We're going in through the back. If Thorne sold us out, someone's waiting for us there."

Rachel nodded, though her eyes showed tension.

— Then let's hope Thorne actually wants to help us.

Nathan didn't have much hope for that.

They entered the mansion through a side entrance Nathan had noticed earlier. The old door leading to the basement was ajar.

Nathan pulled out his flashlight and carefully made his way down the wooden stairs. The basement smelled of damp and dust.

Rachel followed him.

— What exactly are we supposed to find?

"If Langley hid the documents, he must have done it somewhere his children would never see."

Rachel looked at the stacks of dusty crates.

— It could be anywhere.

Nathan walked over to the old desk and began rummaging through the drawers. After a few minutes, he came across something unusual.

— Look at this.

Rachel stepped closer.

an old key in his hands .

"It looks like a bank safety deposit box," Rachel said.

Nathan nodded.

— And there's a number on it.

— Do you think it's here?

Nathan shook his head.

— No. If Langley wanted to hide something, he wouldn't have left it at home. It has to be in the bank.

Rachel looked at him carefully.

— So what now?

Nathan put the key in his pocket.

— We're going back to the city. We need to find the bank that owns that box.

Rachel nodded.

— What if someone already found out about it?

Nathan looked at her seriously.

— Then we have to get there first.

*****

The stolen Lexus, which Nathan had rented under a false name, pulled up outside the Union First Trust Bank in downtown Richmond.

Nathan looked at his watch. It was 6:45 a.m. The bank opened at seven.

Rachel stared at the building.

— What if we need a password?

Nathan smiled slightly.

— We are lawyers. Our job is to convince people that we have the right to be where we shouldn't be.

Rachel sighed.

— Great plan.

When the clock showed seven, they went inside.

Nathan walked up to the counter.

— I would like to access box number 827.

The employee looked at him suspiciously.

— Do you have the key and authorization documents?

Nathan reached into his pocket and pulled out a key.

— I have the key. Documents…

The employee looked at him carefully.

— Whose name is the box in?

Nathan took a deep breath.

—Joseph Langley.

There was silence in the room.

The worker stood up slowly.

— Please wait.

He walked to the back, and Nathan and Rachel exchanged a look.

"Do you think he's calling security?" Rachel asked in a whisper.

Nathan shrugged.

— Or someone worse.

After a moment the employee returned with a short man in a suit.

— My name is David Emerson. I am the director of this department. Please come with me.

Nathan and Rachel followed him down the hallway to the private safety deposit box room.

"Box 827 belongs to Mr. Langley. Our policy is that if you are not the primary owner, we will need proof of authority."

Nathan smiled slightly.

"Mr. Langley's will left all of his assets to my client, Rachel Price.

Emerson looked at Rachel.

— Are you his granddaughter?

Rachel nodded.

— Yes.

Emerson was silent for a moment.

— Please wait here.

Rachel squeezed Nathan's hand.

— I have a bad feeling about this.

— I have them too.

After a while, Emerson returned… with two people in black suits.

— I'm sorry, but we can't provide access to the locker.

Nathan narrowed his eyes.

- Why?

— It has already been emptied.

Rachel turned pale.

- When?

Emerson looked at her.

— This morning.

Nathan felt himself going cold.

— By whom?

Emerson hesitated.

—By Richard Thorne.

Rachel held her breath.

— He betrayed us.

Nathan clenched his fists.

— No, he overtook us .

He turned on his heel and pulled Rachel toward the exit.

"What now?" Rachel asked.

Nathan quickened his pace.

—We'll find Thorne. And we'll find out what he took.

But deep down he knew one thing: if Thorne was part of the deal, they were already a step too late…

*****

Nathan and Rachel raced through the streets of Richmond, trying to find Richard Thorne before it was too late.

"If Thorne had access to the stash, then he was lying from the start," Rachel said, her hands clenching on the passenger seat.

"Or he was playing both sides," Nathan said, passing another set of lights. "We need to find out who he really works for."

Nathan called his detective friend Sam Holloway.

"Sam, I need to find Thorne. Check all the cameras around the bank and see where he went."

"Give me a few minutes," Holloway replied.

Nathan pressed the gas pedal and turned toward Thorne's office.

"If the system didn't know we were looking for these documents, it does now," Rachel said.

"Yes," Nathan agreed. "Which means Thorne just became their biggest problem."

— Do you think they'll eliminate him?

Nathan clenched his jaw.

— If we hurry, we might still be able to find out something from him.

A few minutes later, Holloway called back.

— Thorne left the bank and got into a black Mercedes. He drove south, but—

- But what?

— I lost him. The last time the cameras caught him was in the warehouses on Belle Isle.

— It's a desolate place.

— I know. And it doesn't look like he has an office there.

Nathan glanced at Rachel.

—Maybe he's not looking for an office. Maybe he's looking for a way to disappear.

Nathan hung up and headed toward Belle Isle.

The Belle Isle warehouses were the perfect place to do deals that no one wanted to see. Nathan and Rachel drove up carefully, turning off their lights.

"Are you sure he's here?" Rachel whispered.

Nathan looked at the row of cars parked next to one of the buildings.

— No, but someone is here.

They got out and walked closer. The warehouse was quiet, but Nathan noticed light seeping through a crack in the door.

"What now?" Rachel asked.

— We'll check if Thorne is still alive.

Nathan slowly opened the door and looked inside.

Inside stood several men in suits. In the middle of the room, tied to a chair, sat Richard Thorne .

He had a bloody face and looked beaten. A man with a clean-shaven head, dressed in a black suit, was leaning over him.

"Where are the papers, Richard?" he asked in a calm, icy voice.

Thorne spat on the floor.

— You have no idea what you're getting into, Victor.

Nathan looked at Rachel.

— We have to get him out of there.

Rachel frowned.

— Didn't he just try to trick us?

"Yes," Nathan agreed. "But if they kill him, we lose our last chance to find out what was in those documents."

Rachel looked at the armed men.

— Do you have a plan?

Nathan smiled slightly.

— A bit of improvisation.

He took out his phone and called 911.

"I have a report of a shooting at the Belle Isle warehouses," he said quickly, then hung up.

Rachel looked at him in surprise.

— Do you want to call the police?!

— The police will deal with them. We'll deal with Thorne.

A few seconds later, the first sirens were heard in the distance.

There was a commotion in the warehouse.

"We have a problem," one of the men said.

"Let's get out of here," Victor said.

Nathan knew this was their chance.

As the men in suits began to disperse, he slipped inside and quickly ran over to Thorne.

"If you want to survive, don't move," he whispered.

Thorne looked at him in surprise but didn't protest.

Nathan cut the ropes with the knife on his belt and helped him to his feet.

"We have to get out of here," Rachel said, helping Nathan.

They ran out the back door and jumped into the car.

"Hang in there, Thorne. We're not done talking yet."

*****

Thorne sat in the backseat, breathing heavily.

— You didn't have to save me.

"But we did it. Now tell me where the documents are," Nathan said, looking at him in the mirror.

Thorne wiped blood from his mouth.

— I don't have them.

— You're lying.

Thorne looked at them tiredly.

— I really don't. But I know who does.

Rachel turned to him.

- Who?

Thorne hesitated.

—Eleanor.

Nathan blinked.

— My mother?

— Yes. She never died.

Rachel felt something tighten in her throat.

— Where is she?

Thorne closed his eyes.

— I don't know. But I do know one thing: the system is looking for her.

Nathan picked up his pace.

— So we have to find her first.

Nathan had spent all night analyzing the information. Eleanor Price was alive. This changed everything.

"If the papers are with her, we have an advantage," Rachel said.

— But how do we know where to look for her?

Nathan took a deep breath.

— We'll check her past. We'll find her friends, places where she could be hiding.

Rachel looked at him.

— What if the system finds it first?

Nathan clenched his fists.

— Then it will be too late for all of us.

He knew one thing: the game was getting tougher.

*****

Nathan sat at his desk in his rented hotel suite, looking through files on Eleanor Price. If she was hiding somewhere, they had to find her first.

Rachel sat nearby, staring at her laptop screen. Her eyes flicked through old articles, birth certificates, registry entries.

— My mother hid for forty years. If she wanted to disappear, she had to have help.

"Martin Caldwell," Nathan said. "He helped her then, but now someone's got him. Maybe he told them where Eleanor was."

"So we have two options," Rachel said. "Either we look for her through people she knew…or we try to find people who are already looking for her."

Nathan raised his eyebrows.

— Are you thinking of following the deal?

— Yes. If they already know where he is, then we might be one step behind them … but not two.

Nathan smiled slightly.

— Maybe you're starting to think like a lawyer.

Rachel rolled her eyes.

— I don't know if that's a compliment.

Nathan returned to the laptop.

—Let's see if Martin Caldwell had any properties that could be used as a place of refuge.

Rachel entered his name into the Land and Property Registry. After a moment, she looked at the screen in surprise.

— That's weird.

- What?

Rachel turned the screen towards him.

— Martin Caldwell had a house in North Carolina … but he sold it a year ago.

— To whom?

Rachel clicked on the transaction documents.

—Eleanor Price.

Nathan held his breath.

— We have it.

Six hours later they were on their way to North Carolina.

The house was located in a remote area, near a forest, a few kilometers from a small town where there wasn't even a decent cafe.

Nathan stopped the car in the driveway and looked at Rachel.

— Ready?

Rachel nodded, but there was tension in her eyes.

— What if it's not her?

— We'll find out soon enough.

They got out and went to the door. Nathan knocked.

Silence.

He knocked again.

"Eleanor Price?" he called.

Nothing.

Rachel looked at the windows.

— Maybe she's not here.

Nathan pulled the door handle.

The door was open.

They carefully entered.

The house was small but tidy. On the table was an open book, as if someone had just been reading it.

"Someone lives here," Rachel said quietly.

Nathan walked through the living room and into the kitchen. The sink was empty, but there was a cup of coffee on the counter.

— She was here recently.

Rachel walked over to the bookshelf.

—Nathan…

- What?

Rachel took a framed photo from the shelf and handed it to him.

The photo was of Eleanor Price.

Older, gray hair, but still the same woman they saw in photos from years ago.

Rachel looked at the photo with wide eyes.

— It's really her.

Nathan looked at her.

— Something doesn't seem right here.

Rachel looked at him.

- What?

Nathan pointed to the cup of coffee.

— If she was just here, where is she now?

Then they heard the sound of a door closing.

Rachel turned around sharply.

— There's someone here.

Nathan reached into his pocket for the gun and looked at the stairs leading upstairs.

Someone was there.

And he looked at them.

*****

Rachel felt her heart pounding in her chest.

emerged from the shadows.

She wasn't scared. She wasn't surprised.

She looked at them as if she expected them to come here.

"Eleanor Price?" Nathan asked.

The woman looked at Rachel.

— You are my daughter.

Rachel felt her legs give way beneath her.

— Mom…?

Eleanor nodded.

— I know you've been looking for me.

"Why were you hiding?" Rachel asked.

Eleanor looked at Nathan.

—Because if you found me… that means they found me, too.

Nathan raised his eyebrows.

— They?

Eleanor pressed a finger to her lips.

— There's no time. We have to get out of here.

Rachel looked at her, stunned.

— Mom, what's going on?

Eleanor looked out the window.

— They are already here.

At that moment a bullet hit the window.

"Get down!" Nathan shouted, throwing himself at Rachel to shield her.

Eleanor grabbed her bag from the table and headed for the back exit.

— This way!

Nathan and Rachel ran after her.

In the distance we could hear the screeching of tires and the sound of car doors closing.

"How many are there?" Rachel asked.

Eleanor looked at her seriously.

— Enough to kill us all.

Nathan drew his gun.

— I have a plan.

"What?" Rachel asked.

— We'll run into the forest. We'll have an advantage there.

Eleanor nodded.

— If you want to survive, you have to trust me.

Rachel looked at her mother.

— All my life I've wanted to find you. And now that I have you... I won't let you be lost.

Eleanor squeezed her hand.

— So let's run.

They ran into the darkness, leaving behind their home and the people who wanted to hunt them.

The game is over.

Now it was just about survival.

*****

They ran through the forest, pursued by men who had no intention of leaving them alive. Branches lashed Rachel in the face, but she didn't slow down. Beside her, Eleanor moved surprisingly fast for her age, driven by the instincts that had kept her alive for years.

"How much longer?" Rachel panted.

"A little while longer!" Eleanor replied.

Behind them they heard footsteps, breaking branches, voices.

"Split up!" someone shouted.

Nathan glanced over his shoulder. There were at least four of them, maybe more. All armed.

"If they surround us, we're finished," Nathan said.

"We're not stopping," Eleanor said.

Rachel looked at her mother.

— Where exactly are we running?!

Eleanor didn't answer. A few seconds later they ran into a small clearing.

In the middle was a rusty, abandoned SUV.

"Get in!" Eleanor shouted, pulling the keys out of her pocket.

Rachel looked at her in shock.

— Do you have a car here?!

— You never know when you'll have to run away!

Nathan jumped into the passenger seat, Rachel into the back. Eleanor turned the key.

The engine roared... and stalled.

"Come on, come on..." Eleanor muttered, trying again.

Figures emerged from the darkness.

Nathan raised his gun.

— You have five seconds, Eleanor.

— I'm working on it!

The first shot hit the hood of the car.

"It's now or never!" Rachel shouted.

The engine started.

Eleanor pressed her foot down.

The off-roader took off at full speed, passing a tree and emerging onto a forest road.

"Hang in there!" Eleanor shouted.

Bullets whistled over their heads.

Rachel looked back.

— They have a car!

Nathan reloaded his gun.

— It's gonna be a long night.

They sped down the forest road, the lights of their pursuers blinking in the distance. Rachel glanced at her mother.

— Where are we going?!

"The old motel on the edge of town," Eleanor replied. "I have something there that might help us."

Nathan narrowed his eyes.

— You mean the documents?

Eleanor pursed her lips.

— Something better.

Rachel and Nathan exchanged a look.

— Better?

— Let's just say I have a card up my sleeve they weren't expecting.

Nathan didn't have time to ask what she meant, because at that moment the first car of their pursuers appeared right behind them.

"Hold on!" Eleanor shouted, swerving sharply.

The off-roader veered onto a narrow bridge, but the black SUV behind them did not slow down.

Nathan raised his gun and fired at the tires.

Missed.

"Oh, great!" he muttered.

"Try it again!" Rachel called.

The SUV moved even closer.

Eleanor gritted her teeth.

— Hold on tight!

Suddenly she hit the brakes.

The car slowed down suddenly, the SUV behind them was unable to brake in time and crashed into the bridge railing.

With a screech of tires he flew off the road and crashed into the river.

Rachel looked at it with wide eyes.

— Oh shit.

Nathan looked at Eleanor.

— Are you sure you weren't an FBI agent at one time?

Eleanor smiled slightly.

— I was a nurse. But life taught me a few tricks.

Eleanor pressed the accelerator.

— We've got about five minutes of advantage left before the rest of them catch up.

"Is that enough?" Rachel asked.

— It's enough if the motel is where I left it.

Nathan raised his eyebrows.

- If?

Eleanor smiled slightly.

- We'll see.

*****

The Red Pine Motel looked like something that should have been closed a decade ago. Its neon sign was flickering and the parking lot was nearly empty.

Eleanor backed the car up to one of the rooms and got out first.

— Come on.

Nathan and Rachel followed her.

Eleanor opened the door to room 107.

It was stuffy inside, with just an old bed, a 90s TV, and a scuffed chest of drawers.

"Is this supposed to help us?" Rachel asked skeptically.

Eleanor walked over to the wall and began to feel the wallpaper.

— No. It does.

She pressed one point on the wall and the wallpaper lifted slightly.

Behind it was a small safe.

Nathan looked at her with admiration.

— We need to talk about your past.

Eleanor entered the code and opened the safe.

She took out a thick stack of papers and threw it on the bed.

Rachel picked up the first page.

- What is this?

Nathan leaned closer.

Names.

Politicians. Judges. Wall Street types. Anyone connected to Langley.

Eleanor looked at them seriously.

— This is a list of people who have been part of the system for decades.

Nathan flipped through the pages.

— Bribery… rigged contracts…

Rachel stared at one particular name.

- God…

Nathan looked at her.

- What?

Rachel swallowed hard.

— Richard Thorne is on the list.

Nathan took the paper and looked at it carefully.

— And that means one thing.

Rachel looked at him.

- What?

Nathan gripped the paper tighter.

—That Thorne didn't work for the system.

Rachel frowned.

— How so?

Nathan looked at Eleanor.

— He tried to destroy them.

Eleanor nodded.

— Yes. And that's why the system got him.

Rachel looked at the documents in horror.

— If this comes to light, it will sweep away the entire world of politics and business in the United States.

Nathan put the pages aside and looked at Eleanor.

— The question is... what now?

Eleanor picked up the gun she had hidden in the safe.

—Now we must do what Joseph Langley never had the courage to do.

Nathan looked at her carefully.

— Reveal everything.

Nathan closed the safe and looked at Rachel and Eleanor.

"If this list is real, we have more than just a will. We have a gun."

Rachel looked at the papers scattered on the bed.

— This isn't just a list of names. This is evidence of crimes that could destroy people at the highest levels of government.

Eleanor took one of the documents and pointed to the signature at the bottom of the page.

— Do you see this?

Nathan looked at the name.

Senator Mitchell Crane.

Rachel narrowed her eyes.

— He's about to be nominated to the Supreme Court.

"And if this document sees the light of day, his career will be over," Nathan said.

Eleanor picked up another paper.

— Not just him. The list includes people from Congress, federal judges, CEOs of major banks.

Rachel swallowed hard.

— Which means they all have a reason to silence us.

Nathan put down the papers and looked at Eleanor.

— If you had it all along, why did you never reveal it?

Eleanor sighed.

—Because I knew if I did, the system would find me.

Rachel looked at her carefully.

— And now?

Eleanor looked her daughter in the eye.

— I have no choice now.

Nathan glanced at his watch.

— We have to hurry. If these people know we have these documents, they won't stop chasing us.

Rachel took a deep breath.

— So what now?

Nathan looked at her seriously.

— Now we need to find someone to pass this on to.

*****

They knew one thing: they couldn't go to the police.

Nathan had a few friends in the FBI, but the list included the names of several high-ranking agents.

"If we give this to the wrong person, we'll die," Nathan said.

Eleanor got up and went to the window.

— There is one person we can trust.

Rachel looked at her.

- Who?

Eleanor turned to them.

—Michael Hayes.

Nathan raised his eyebrows.

— Investigative journalist?

Eleanor nodded.

— If we want these documents to see the light of day, we need someone who knows how to use them.

Rachel looked at Nathan.

— Is that a good idea?

Nathan thought for a moment.

"Hayes has a reputation for not being afraid of big things. The establishment won't be able to silence him easily."

— So are we going to him?

Eleanor reached for her bag of documents.

— Yes. But we have to hurry.

Nathan got up and took out his phone.

— I'll call him and arrange a meeting.

Rachel looked out the window.

— What if they already know what we're planning?

Nathan looked at her.

— Then we'll have to fight.

They arranged to meet Hayes at a small restaurant on the outskirts of Washington.

Hayes was cautious. He told them to leave their phones in the car and sit in the back of the venue, away from the windows.

When he finally appeared, he was wearing a simple shirt and sunglasses.

"I don't know what exactly you have, but if you're calling me in the middle of the night, it must be something serious," he said, sitting up.

Nathan took out a briefcase and handed him the documents.

— This is more than just a big case. This is evidence of a system that has controlled American politics for the past four decades.

Hayes glanced at the front page and his face immediately became serious.

- God…

Rachel leaned closer.

— Can you publish it?

Hayes looked at them carefully.

— If I do this, my life won't be the same.

Eleanor looked at him coldly.

— Your life won't be the same anyway. If the system finds out you had those documents in your hands, you'll be a target.

Hayes was silent for a long moment.

— Do you have copies?

Nathan nodded.

— Two. One is safe.

Hayes took a deep breath.

"Give me some time. I need to look this over and make sure everything is correct."

Rachel looked at Nathan.

— What if the system finds out about this?

Nathan turned to Hayes.

— If we're going to do this, we need to act quickly.

Hayes looked at them and nodded.

— Then there is no turning back.

He stood up, put his documents in his bag and headed towards the exit.

Then the first shot was fired.

Hayes fell to the ground, holding his arm.

"Get out of here!" Nathan shouted, diving behind the table.

Rachel pulled Eleanor along with her.

People in the restaurant started screaming and running away.

Nathan glanced out the window.

There was a black SUV on the street and armed men were getting out of it.

"We have a problem!" he shouted.

Rachel looked at Hayes, who was struggling to get to his feet.

— Are you alive?

Hayes gritted his teeth.

— A scratch. But that means they knew we'd be here.

Nathan looked at Eleanor.

— We have to get out.

Eleanor looked around.

— There's a back exit.

Nathan glanced toward the kitchen.

— We are running.

They got up and started moving. Bullets hit the walls, smashed plates, and shattered windows.

Nathan opened the back door and they ran out into the parking lot.

"The car's on the other side," Rachel said.

But then the door on the street side opened and two men stepped out.

One of them raised his gun.

— End of the road, Mr. Bishop.

Nathan looked at Rachel and Eleanor.

They were trapped.

Nathan raised his hands, staring at the two armed men standing between them and freedom. Rachel squeezed her mother's hand, feeling her heart pound.

Michael Hayes, despite the bullet grazing his arm, was still holding the bag of documents.

"Hand over your papers," one of the attackers said, aiming a gun at Hayes.

"If you think you can stop this, you're dumber than you look," Hayes said, trying to buy time.

The second attacker took a step closer.

— It wasn't a request.

Nathan glanced at Rachel and Eleanor. They couldn't let those documents fall into the wrong hands.

"Okay, calm down," he said, raising his hand. "We can work this out."

The first attacker raised his weapon higher.

— There are no negotiations.

Nathan saw the other one glance toward the street for a moment, as if checking to see if they were alone. This was his chance.

Before anyone could react, Nathan lunged at the nearest attacker. He grabbed his wrist and swung the gun to the side. The shot bounced off the asphalt next to his foot.

Rachel screamed as the second attacker aimed at Nathan.

Then Eleanor reached for the knife she had in her pocket and threw it into his hand.

The man screamed and his gun fell to the ground.

Nathan landed a punch in the face of the first attacker, knocking him to his knees.

Rachel ran up to the other one and kicked his gun away.

"Get in the car!" Nathan shouted.

Hayes, despite his pain, opened the door and climbed inside. Eleanor and Rachel jumped in after him.

Nathan got into the driver's seat, started the engine, and screeched out of the parking lot.

"Where are we going?!" Rachel shouted.

Nathan looked at Hayes.

— Do you have a place we can hide?

Hayes, breathing heavily, pulled out his phone.

— Yes. But if we want to expose it, we have to act quickly.

Nathan nodded.

— Then call.

*****

They hid in a small, isolated cottage belonging to Hayes, a few miles outside of town.

Rachel bandaged the journalist's arm while Nathan and Eleanor discussed the next step.

"The establishment already knows these documents are in play," Nathan said. "Now they'll do anything to silence us."

Eleanor looked tired as she sat on the couch, but her eyes were full of determination.

— We can't stop now. These papers must reach the public.

Hayes, though still dazed by pain, looked at them.

"I have an editor friend at The Washington Post. If we can get into their office, I can give it to them."

Rachel looked at Nathan.

— This is our only chance.

Nathan nodded.

— But we can't go straight to them. They'll be watching us.

Eleanor leaned forward.

— There is another way.

Nathan looked at her questioningly.

- What?

Eleanor took a deep breath.

"My friend Sarah Whitmore worked at the Justice Department. She was one of the few people who knew the story of my father and the arrangement. If anyone can help us get this out there and protect us, it's her."

Nathan looked at Hayes.

— Can we trust her?

Hayes nodded.

"If this is the same Sarah Whitmore I think she is, then she is clean."

Rachel looked at her mother.

— What if the system has already found it?

Eleanor clenched her fists.

— Then we are on our own.

Nathan stood up.

— There's no time to speculate. We're going to Washington.

*****

The drive to Washington was quiet. Each of them knew this was the home stretch.

Nathan drove on back roads, avoiding main roads to avoid detection.

Eleanor stared at the city lights passing by.

— For forty years I lived in the shadow. I ran away, changed identities. And all the time I was afraid that one day they would find me.

Rachel looked at her.

— And now?

Eleanor turned to her daughter.

— There is no turning back now.

Nathan turned into a narrow street.

— Whitmore's address is 1801 Wisconsin Avenue. But if the system has already gotten to her, we have to be ready for anything.

Rachel looked at Hayes.

— Can you do it?

The journalist, even though he looked pale, smiled slightly.

— I've worked on big cases. But this is the biggest.

Nathan slowed down and stopped the car in front of the building.

— It's here.

They got out carefully and moved towards the door.

Nathan knocked.

Silence.

He tried again.

Nothing.

Rachel looked at her mother.

— Maybe she's not here?

Eleanor looked out the window.

— The light is on. She's here.

Nathan checked the door handle.

The door was open.

He looked at Eleanor and Rachel.

— Something is wrong here.

They slowly walked inside.

The living room looked normal, but there was a broken cup on the table and an overturned chair on the floor.

Rachel felt a knot in her stomach.

- God…

Nathan took a step deeper into the apartment.

— Sarah?

Then he saw something that made his heart stop.

On the wall, someone wrote one sentence in blood.

"STOP WHILE YOU STILL CAN."

Rachel covered her mouth with her hand.

— Is that...?

Eleanor stared at the wall, pale as paper.

— This is their warning.

Nathan looked at her.

— Not just a warning. It's a message.

Rachel looked at him.

- What do you mean?

Nathan clenched his jaw.

— That means they've already found us.

*****

Nathan stared at the red letters on the wall. The words " STOP WHILE YOU STILL CAN " looked like a sentence.

Rachel breathed heavily as she looked at the signs of struggle in the room.

— Do you think Sarah…?

Nathan was still staring at the sign.

"I don't know. But if they took her alive, that means they still have some use for her."

Eleanor touched the marks on the floor.

— The blood is still fresh. It happened recently.

Hayes, pale as a sheet, leaned against the dresser.

"We have to get out of here. If the system left us a message, that means they know where we are."

Nathan looked at Eleanor.

— Is there anywhere else we can hide?

Eleanor pondered.

— There is one. But it's risky.

Rachel looked at her.

— How much?

Eleanor looked her daughter in the eye.

— We have to go back to my father's house.

Nathan frowned.

— To the Langley residence?

Eleanor nodded.

— That's where it started. And that's where it'll end.

*****

The drive to the Langley estate was quiet. Rachel stared out the window, trying to comprehend how her life had changed over the past few days.

Nathan focused on the road, but his thoughts were elsewhere.

"If the system already knows we have the documents, why are they still warning us?" he said quietly.

Hayes, sitting in the backseat, looked at him wearily.

— Because they still lack something.

Rachel looked at Eleanor.

— What else are you hiding?

Eleanor sighed.

— I'm not hiding anything. But it's possible that there's something in my father's house that they still haven't found.

Nathan tightened his hands on the steering wheel.

— So let's check it out.

The Langley Manor loomed around the bend, the building standing somberly among the tall trees as if it still held secrets.

Nathan stopped the car a few hundred yards from the gate.

"We can't just go in there. If they're watching us..."

"Then they know we're here," Eleanor finished.

Rachel looked at her mother.

— So what do we do?

Eleanor reached into the glove compartment of her car and pulled out a small revolver.

— We're going in.

*****

They entered through a side door. The interior was dark and quiet, but Nathan sensed they were not alone.

Eleanor led them through the corridors until they reached the old library.

"What's here?" Rachel asked.

Eleanor walked over to one of the shelves and began moving books around.

"My father had a safe here. If he didn't take all his secrets to the grave, the answer might be there."

Nathan helped her find a hidden panel. A moment later, she uncovered a small metal safe built into the wall.

Eleanor took a deep breath and entered the code.

The lock clicked.

Nathan looked at Eleanor.

— Are you sure you want to see this?

Eleanor looked into his eyes.

— I've been afraid of that safe my whole life. It's time to find out the truth.

She opened the door and pulled out a briefcase.

Rachel looked at the stack of documents.

- What is this?

Eleanor spread the papers on the table.

The first page had the headline:

"OPERATION CYCLOP"

Nathan raised his eyebrows.

— What the hell is this?

Hayes took one of the pieces of paper and began to read.

— These look like… operational reports.

Rachel glanced at the title page.

— What does "Tick..." mean?

Suddenly Eleanor turned pale.

- God.

Nathan looked at her.

- What?

Eleanor clutched the papers.

— It wasn't just a political arrangement. It was an organization of killers.

There was silence.

Rachel stared at her mother.

— Do you mean to say that...?

Eleanor nodded.

—My father's men didn't just control politicians. They eliminated those who threatened them.

Nathan flipped through the pages.

— It's a list of operations. Attacks, deaths ruled as accidents… God, those names…

Hayes nodded.

— Many of these cases were considered unsolved.

Rachel closed her eyes.

— So it's not just about money. It's about power.

Nathan looked at Eleanor.

— Why does the system still pursue you?

Eleanor took a deep breath.

— Because I'm the last person who knows the truth.

Rachel looked at the documents.

— That's all ... if we reveal this, it's over for them.

Hayes nodded.

— But we have to do it quickly.

Nathan raised his head.

— Then we can't send it to the press. It has to go to someone who has real power.

Eleanor looked at him.

— To whom?

Nathan took a deep breath.

— To someone who is not part of the arrangement.

Rachel frowned.

— Is there anyone like that?

Nathan smiled slightly.

— Yes. And I know where to find him.

*****

Nathan parked in front of a monumental building in downtown Washington.

Rachel glanced at the sign at the entrance.

— Department of Justice?

Nathan nodded.

— If we have anyone who can stop this, it's the Attorney General.

Hayes looked at him skeptically.

— Are you sure he's not part of the deal?

Nathan opened the door.

— Let's find out.

They went inside. The guards looked at them, but Nathan showed his attorney ID.

— We have an appointment.

The secretary led them to the office.

Sitting behind the desk was Attorney General Richard Calloway.

He looked at them calmly.

— How can I help?

Nathan walked closer and placed the papers on the desk.

"This is proof of the system that has controlled this country for decades. If you want to stop it, now's your chance."

Calloway looked at the papers.

He raised his head.

He smiled slightly.

— I was waiting for someone to bring it…

Nathan looked into the smiling face of Attorney General Richard Calloway. The room fell silent, broken only by the soft chime of the clock on the desk.

Rachel exchanged a quick glance with Eleanor, and Michael Hayes, though pale from blood loss, sat up straight as if ready for another fight.

"Were you waiting for these documents?" Nathan repeated slowly.

Calloway nodded and spread the papers out on his desk, turning the pages with the caution of a man who had just held in his hands the potential end of the political careers of many powerful men.

— I knew something like this existed. I had my suspicions, but I never had proof.

Nathan crossed his arms.

— And now you have them.

Calloway looked up and looked at him carefully.

— You don't think it's that simple, do you?

Rachel clenched her hands.

— We have evidence. We can release it.

Calloway sighed and leaned back in his chair.

"Miss Price, you don't know how the world works. This isn't a movie. This isn't a newspaper article that's going to turn everything upside down. The system you're talking about has worked for decades. That means it has loyal people everywhere. "

Eleanor spoke for the first time.

— So you're not going to do anything about it?

Calloway looked at her carefully.

— I didn't say that.

He reached for the telephone on his desk and pressed a button.

— Heather, please close my schedule for the rest of the day. And don't let anyone in.

"Yes, Mr. Prosecutor," the secretary's voice replied.

Nathan glanced at Eleanor.

— Does that mean you're with us?

Calloway sighed.

— That means I have to make a damn hard decision.

*****

Calloway looked through the documents for almost an hour.

Rachel was pacing around the room nervously, Nathan was sitting in an armchair, and Eleanor was staring out the window as if she expected someone to break in at any moment.

Finally, Calloway closed the briefcase and looked at them.

— We can go ahead with this. But it will be a war.

Nathan raised his eyebrows.

- War?

Calloway looked him straight in the eye.

"You can't think these people are just going to let us press charges. If we go to court, they'll intimidate witnesses, bribe judges, destroy evidence. And if that's not enough, they'll do worse."

Eleanor spoke quietly.

— I know what they are capable of.

Calloway sighed.

— We need a strategy. We can't go into this blindly.

Michael Hayes, who had been silent until now, spoke up.

— I know a few people in the media. If we get this out there faster than the system can react, their defenses could fall apart.

Calloway looked at him.

— And you think the media will protect you?

Hayes shrugged.

— If information reaches millions of people at the same time, it cannot be taken back.

Nathan nodded.

— What if we divide the evidence?

Calloway raised his eyebrows.

— What did you come up with?

Nathan looked at each of them in turn.

"Instead of sending everything to one place, we'll send these documents to different newsrooms, government agencies, and international organizations. If it goes to different sources at once, the system won't be able to stop everything at once."

Calloway looked at him carefully.

— This is madness.

— Maybe. But it's the only chance.

Eleanor nodded.

— We are doing it.

The next hours were full of tension.

Nathan and Rachel sent scans of the documents to journalists, international anti-corruption organizations, and even several senators known for fighting political corruption.

Hayes called his contact at The Washington Post.

"This could be the biggest case of the last thirty years," he said on the phone.

Calloway held an internal meeting at the Justice Department, selecting only the most trusted people.

At 11:45 pm the first articles began appearing online.

The headlines said it all:

"A SECRET ORGANIZATION RULES THE COUNTRY? NEW DOCUMENTS ARE SHOCKING"

"HIDDEN CRIMES OF POWER – WHO IS BEHIND THE CORRUPTION SYSTEM?"

"LANGLEY RESIDENCE DOCUMENTS: CONSPIRATIONS, MURDER, BRIBERY"

Rachel stared at her phone screen, watching the news spread like wildfire.

"We did it…" she whispered.

Nathan looked at Calloway.

— What now?

The Attorney General reached for the telephone.

— I'm now preparing federal arrest warrants.

*****

The first arrests took place at dawn.

Senator Mitchell Crane was led from the house in handcuffs.

The vice president of one of the country's largest banks was detained at the airport while trying to escape on a private jet.

The list of names went on forever.

Rachel and Eleanor watched the live broadcast in their hotel room.

"I can't believe this is actually happening..." Rachel said.

Eleanor smiled slightly.

— Your grandfather was afraid the truth would never come out. But you revealed it.

Rachel looked at her mother.

— Is it over?

Eleanor shook her head.

— This is just the beginning.

At that moment Nathan returned to the room, newspaper in hand.

— We have a problem.

Rachel looked at him worriedly.

- What?

Nathan threw the newspaper on the table.

The headline was:

"MYSTERIOUS DISAPPEARANCE OF ATTORNEY GENERAL. CALLAWAY FAILED TO REPORT TO OFFICE"

Rachel frowned.

- What?!

Nathan nodded.

— He left his apartment last night and disappeared without a trace.

Eleanor tightened her grip on her coffee cup.

— The system strikes back.

Rachel looked at Nathan.

— So what do we do?

Nathan looked at the newspaper.

— We find Calloway. Before it's too late.

*****

Nathan sat at his laptop, searching the city's surveillance system. Michael Hayes, who had joined them, was turning pages in a notebook.

"Did Calloway have protection?" Hayes asked.

"Yes," Nathan replied. "But two of his bodyguards were found dead in their car."

Rachel felt a shiver run down her spine.

— So it wasn't an ordinary kidnapping.

Eleanor looked at the screen.

—What if Calloway managed to say something before he disappeared?

Nathan frowned.

- What do you mean?

Eleanor picked up the phone and called her old contact at the Justice Department. A moment later, a voice answered on the other end.

— Sarah, this is Eleanor. I need some information.

— You know that after this case everyone is angry at you, right?

"I know. But it can't end. Calloway's gone."

There was silence on the other end.

"What do you know?" Eleanor pressed.

— He was in contact with someone. He met with them just before he disappeared.

Nathan leaned closer to the phone.

- With whom?

—With Supreme Court Justice Charles Whitmore.

Rachel looked at Eleanor.

-Whitmore... He's Sarah's brother.

Eleanor nodded.

"If Calloway told him something, we need to meet with him."

Hayes looked at Nathan.

—Do you think Whitmore can help us?

Nathan took a deep breath.

— If he's still alive.

*****

Nathan and Rachel waited in a dark car outside Judge Whitmore's residence. It was two in the morning, and the street was empty.

"Do you think the system knows we're looking for him, too?" Rachel asked.

"If they know Calloway talked to him, Whitmore is their next target," Nathan said.

Rachel looked at her phone.

— If we are to warn him, we need to act now.

Nathan looked at Eleanor and Hayes.

— Let's go.

They walked up to the door. Nathan knocked.

Silence.

He knocked again.

Nothing.

"That's not a good sign," Rachel said.

Nathan reached into his pocket and pulled out a skeleton key.

— I feel like we don't have a choice anyway.

A few seconds later the door opened and they walked in.

The house was dark.

There was an overturned armchair in the living room, just like in Sarah Whitmore's apartment.

Nathan drew his gun.

— Something is wrong here.

Then Rachel screamed.

- Oh my God...

On the wall, in red paint, someone wrote:

"IT'S TOO LATE."

Beneath lay the body of Charles Whitmore.

Rachel fell to her knees.

- NO…

Eleanor ran to her and put her arm around her.

Nathan looked at Hayes, who turned even paler.

— The arrangement was already here.

Hayes looked at the blood smeared on the floor.

— What if they left something behind?

Nathan walked closer to Whitmore's body and saw something sticking out of his jacket.

Flash drive.

He took it out gently and looked at Rachel.

— Maybe this is the key.

Rachel was still looking at the dead judge.

— And if not?

Eleanor looked at Nathan.

— That means we're next.

*****

Nathan inserted the flash drive into the laptop in the hotel room. The file only had one folder.

It was called "Calloway's Last Message."

Nathan clicked.

A recording appeared on the screen.

Calloway sat in the dark room, talking rapidly, nervously.

"If you're watching this, it means they got me. The establishment knew I was gathering evidence. Whitmore was the last person I could trust."

Nathan looked at Rachel and Eleanor.

Calloway continued.

"There's another name. The man who stands at the top. He never showed up in the documents, never left any traces. But I found evidence. He's the architect of it all."

Rachel held her breath.

Calloway looked directly into the camera.

— His name is William Royce.

Nathan froze.

- NO…

Hayes looked at him.

— Do you know him?

Nathan nodded slowly.

—Royce… is a leading candidate to be the next President of the United States.

Rachel looked at the screen, feeling a cold shiver run down her spine.

— If this is true... it means that the arrangement never fell through.

Nathan took a deep breath.

— No. It means that we are just beginning the real war.

*****

Nathan turned off the recording and looked at Rachel, Eleanor, and Hayes.

—William Royce.

Rachel swallowed hard.

— The man who will probably become president of the United States in a year.

Hayes rested his hands on the table, staring at his laptop.

"If Royce is indeed the architect of the arrangement, then we are dealing with someone who has unlimited power, unlimited resources, and people at every level of government.

Nathan looked at the flash drive in his hand.

"Calloway said he had evidence. We need to find where he hid it."

Eleanor spoke quietly:

— And if he didn't make it?

Nathan looked into her eyes.

— That means we have to find them ourselves.

Rachel stood up and began to pace nervously around the room.

"After we leaked the Langley documents, Royce knows we're a threat. He'll be looking for us "

Hayes looked at Nathan.

— Do you have any other contacts who could help us?

Nathan reached for his phone and searched through his notes.

— There is one person. A former CIA agent who once investigated Royce.

Rachel looked at him.

— Do you think he knows something?

"I know Royce ruined his career when he was close to finding out the truth. If anyone has a clue, it's him."

Hayes crossed his arms.

— Who is this man?

Nathan looked at them seriously.

—Jonathan Slate.

*****

Jonathan Slate lived in a small, run-down house on the outskirts of Philadelphia. When Nathan knocked on the door, there was a moment of silence.

Finally, they heard a voice from behind the door.

— If you're from the FBI, then let me tell you right away that I have lawyers.

Nathan exchanged a look with Rachel and Eleanor.

"Slate, it's me, Nathan Bishop. We need to talk."

A moment of silence.

— Bishop? What the hell are you doing here?

— It's a long story, but if you don't let us in, we won't have time to tell it.

The lock clicked and the door swung open.

Slate looked like a man who had long ago resigned himself to life on the margins. His hair was streaked with gray, his face tired.

"Come in," he murmured, closing the door behind them.

They sat down in his living room. There were papers everywhere, empty whiskey bottles, and boxes of unopened mail.

"So?" Slate leaned back in his chair and looked at Nathan. "What's so important you came all the way here?"

Nathan put the flash drive on the table.

— It's about William Royce.

Slate looked at the carrier, then at Nathan.

— Jesus Christ…

Rachel leaned forward.

— You know him, right?

Slate burst out laughing.

—Of course, I know him. He ruined my life.

Eleanor looked at him carefully.

- What happened?

Slate took a deep breath.

— In 2009, I was running an operation in South America. We were tracking a financial network connected to American politicians. It all led back to Royce.

Nathan stared at him.

— But you never managed to get him.

Slate shook his head.

"No. Because before I could present my evidence, I was accused of working with the cartels. Money was planted in my account; fake phone records were made. The CIA threw me out, the FBI opened an investigation. All to keep Royce clean."

Rachel narrowed her eyes.

— And you just gave up?

Slate looked at her sharply.

— I had no choice.

Nathan took the flash drive.

"Calloway left evidence here, but we don't know where the physical documents might be."

Slate was silent for a moment.

"If Royce was actually running a deal, he would never have kept the evidence in an obvious place."

Nathan looked at Eleanor.

— But if he had protection...?

Eleanor nodded.

—Every paranoid keeps a copy in case they need to protect themselves.

Slate nodded.

—Royce had one man he trusted most. James Holloway.

Hayes looked at Slate in surprise.

— Holloway? Former national security advisor?

"Yeah. If Royce had a copy somewhere, Holloway knows where to find it."

Nathan clenched his fists.

— And where is he now?

Slate looked at them seriously.

— Runs the Global Future Foundation in New York.

Rachel raised her eyebrows.

— The Foundation?

Slate smiled bitterly.

— Best place to hide dirty money.

Nathan stood up.

— So we're going to New York.

Slate looked at him doubtfully.

— If you think you can just walk in and ask for documents, you are naive.

Nathan looked him straight in the eye.

— And if anyone needs to ask that question, it's us.

*****

Nathan and Rachel stood in the elegant lobby of a building belonging to Global Future.

Eleanor and Hayes were waiting in the car a few blocks away, ready to act if anything went wrong.

The receptionist looked at them coldly.

— Do you have an appointment?

Nathan smiled slightly.

— Yes. With Mr. Holloway.

The receptionist glanced at the monitor.

— I don't see such a meeting here.

Rachel looked at Nathan.

— Do you think he'll let us in?

Nathan leaned against the counter and looked directly at the receptionist.

"Please tell Mr. Holloway we have information about William Royce.

The receptionist paused for a moment, then reached for the telephone.

Nathan looked at Rachel.

— If they know we're here, they're already watching us.

Rachel felt a shiver.

— So what now?

Nathan looked toward the hallway.

— We are waiting.

The elevator doors opened quietly.

entered the lobby.

He looked at them coldly.

— Well… I thought you would never come here.

*****

James Holloway entered the lobby with the confidence of a man always in control. The former national security adviser, now head of one of the most powerful foundations in the world, looked like someone who never lost his cool.

Nathan and Rachel exchanged a quick look.

"I thought you'd never show up here," Holloway repeated, stepping closer.

"Well, maybe it's time for some answers," Nathan replied.

Holloway looked them over, then looked at the receptionist.

— Tell them I don't want anyone to disturb us.

"Yes, Mr. Holloway," the woman said, looking at them worriedly.

Holloway turned to them and gestured for them to enter the elevator.

— All right, come on.

Nathan hesitated for a split second, then moved after him. Rachel did the same, feeling tension tighten in her stomach.

As the elevator doors closed behind them, Holloway looked at them and smiled slightly.

— What you are about to do could turn this country upside down.

Nathan crossed his arms.

— We know.

Holloway nodded.

— Good. Because if you make one mistake, Royce and his men will crush you like insects.

Rachel narrowed her eyes.

— And you want to help us?

Holloway looked at her carefully.

— Maybe. But first I need to know if you're ready for the consequences.

The elevator doors opened onto a luxurious office on the top floor of the building.

"Come on in," Holloway said, leading them inside.

Nathan and Rachel entered the spacious office, and Holloway went to the bar and poured himself a whiskey.

— Would you like a drink?

"I would prefer answers," Nathan said.

Holloway smiled slightly and sat down on the leather couch.

— Okay. Let's start with the most important question: What exactly do you want from me?

*****

Rachel sat in the chair across from Holloway.

— We know Royce is the architect of the arrangement. We know that for decades he has built a network of people who control politics, finances and the justice system.

Nathan leaned forward slightly.

—We need evidence. And we know that if anyone has it, it's you.

Holloway smiled and raised his glass to his lips.

"So you found me because you believe I have something that can destroy Royce."

"We don't believe it," Nathan corrected him. "We know it"

Holloway nodded, setting down his glass.

— You're smart. And maybe you even have the courage to fight him. But let me ask you straight…

He leaned forward and his eyes became cold and inscrutable.

— Are you ready to kill someone?

Rachel held her breath.

- What?

Holloway looked at her without blinking.

"Royce won't let you go. If you want to stop him, you'll have to go further than you think."

Nathan tensed his muscles.

— We don't kill people.

Holloway smiled slightly.

- Still.

Rachel looked at Nathan, then at Holloway.

— You know him. You know where the evidence is.

Holloway looked at her seriously.

- Yes, I know.

Nathan leaned closer.

- Where?

Holloway smiled slightly.

— That's why you're here.

*****

Holloway stood up and walked to the wall. He pressed a hidden button, and a wall panel slid open, revealing a safe.

Rachel held her breath.

Holloway entered the code and the safe door opened.

Inside there was a black briefcase.

Holloway took it out and placed it on the table.

Nathan opened the briefcase and looked at the contents.

— These are…

Rachel looked at the documents.

— Financial transactions. Secret agreements.

Nathan took out one of the magazines.

Holloway looked at them.

— That's all you need to destroy him.

Rachel looked at him carefully.

— Why are you giving this to us?

Holloway shrugged.

"Because Royce is no longer the man I knew. He's become too powerful. And men like him shouldn't have absolute power."

Nathan closed the briefcase.

"If Royce finds out about this, we're dead."

Holloway smiled slightly.

— So, don't let him find out.

Rachel looked at Nathan.

— What now?

Nathan took a deep breath.

— Now we need to hand it over to someone who will do what needs to be done with it.

Holloway looked at them carefully.

— So… I have one last name for you.

Rachel held her breath.

— Who?

Holloway leaned over them and said quietly:

—Robert Kingsley.

Nathan frowned.

—The FBI director?

Holloway nodded.

— If anyone can dismantle this system from the inside, it's him. But you'll have to hurry.

Rachel looked at Nathan.

— If Royce finds out we have these documents…

Holloway looked at her seriously.

— He already found out.

Nathan looked at the door.

— We have to run. Now.

*****

Nathan, Rachel, and Holloway looked at each other at the same time.

"What do you mean Royce already found out?" Nathan asked.

Holloway glanced at his watch.

— Because if I knew you would come here, then he did too.

Rachel looked toward the window.

— Shit…

Two black SUVs stopped on the street in front of the building.

Nathan took a deep breath.

— So this is a trap?

Holloway shook his head.

— No. It's a test.

Rachel looked at him sharply.

— Test?!

Holloway walked over to the desk and took a gun out of the drawer.

"Royce wants to see what you'll do when he finds you."

Nathan looked at the door.

— If we don't escape now, we won't have a second chance.

Holloway handed him the gun.

— You won't get out of the elevator. But I have another option.

Nathan looked at him.

- What?

Holloway smiled slightly.

— Roof.

*****

They ran down the hallway leading to the roof. A security alarm sounded throughout the building.

"How much time do we have?" Rachel asked, trying to keep up with Nathan.

"A minute or two until they get to us," Nathan replied.

Holloway ran after them, gun in hand.

— I've got a helicopter on the roof. It can take us to another part of town.

Nathan glanced at him.

— Do you have a helicopter?

Holloway shrugged.

— This is New York. Rich people don't like sitting in traffic jams.

They reached the door leading to the roof.

Nathan opened it and saw a helicopter, its rotors already turning.

— Come on!

They ran onto the landing pad. Rachel looked back.

Four armed men appeared in the corridor.

"They're shooting!" she screamed.

Nathan hid behind a metal container, pulled out his gun and fired several shots.

Holloway looked at the pilots.

— Take off!

The helicopter's engines roared as the plane began to rise above the ground.

Rachel, Nathan, and Holloway ran aboard.

One of Royce's men aimed directly at Rachel.

Nathan threw himself at her, shielding her with his own body.

A shot was fired.

*****

Rachel felt an impact, but she wasn't sure if it was the bullet or the force with which Nathan pushed her.

The helicopter took off as the city began to recede beneath them.

"Nathan!" Rachel looked at him as he fell to the floor of the cabin.

There was a stain of blood on his shirt.

"Shit…" he hissed, pressing his hand to his side.

Holloway knelt next to him.

"It doesn't look fatal. But if we don't stop the bleeding, it'll get worse."

Rachel grabbed a first aid kit from inside the helicopter and began dressing the wound.

Nathan looked at her with a weak smile.

— You're a pretty good nurse.

"Shut up and don't die," Rachel said.

Holloway looked at the pilot.

— We're changing our route. We're going to a government shelter in Virginia.

Nathan looked at him in disbelief.

— Do you have access to a CIA safe house?

Holloway smiled.

— Royce isn't the only one with secrets.

The helicopter flew towards Virginia.

Rachel looked at Nathan, squeezing his hand.

—You can't die now. Not after everything.

Nathan smiled slightly.

— So, we need to finish this matter.

*****

The CIA shelter was located in a remote area, in an old mansion that looked like an ordinary house.

When they arrived, Nathan could barely stand.

Rachel and Holloway helped him inside, where the doctor was already waiting for them.

"Take care of him," Holloway said, and the doctor took Nathan to a separate room.

Rachel sat down on the sofa and hid her face in her hands.

Eleanor entered the room.

— Are you okay?

Rachel looked at her mother.

—Nathan was shot.

Eleanor glanced toward the closed door behind which the doctor was dressing his wound.

— He'll survive. He's stronger than you think.

Rachel took a breath and looked at Holloway.

— What now?

Holloway sat down across from her.

— If Royce already knows we have the documents, it means he's preparing for a counterattack.

Rachel narrowed her eyes.

— What if we overtake him?

Holloway smiled slightly.

— That's exactly what I was thinking.

Rachel looked at Eleanor.

— We have to do what we wanted to do before. But this time we're going to strike at the heart of the system.

Holloway looked at them.

— What do you mean?

Rachel took a deep breath.

— We're calling a press conference. And we're telling the whole world the truth about Royce.

*****

The next day, Holloway used his contacts to gather journalists at a secret location.

Rachel stood in front of the cameras, Eleanor next to her.

Nathan, even though he was weakened from being shot, sat down next to Hayes.

The spotlight turned on Rachel, who took a deep breath.

— Thank you for coming. I have news to share today that will shake this country.

The reporters began to whisper among themselves.

Rachel looked directly at the cameras.

— William Royce is not the man he claims to be. He is the creator of a corruption network that has manipulated the politics and economy of the United States for decades.

There was silence.

Rachel picked up a stack of papers.

— And here is the evidence.

Cameras began to record every detail.

Nathan looked at Eleanor.

— It's over for Royce.

Eleanor nodded.

— I hope you're right.

At that moment the conference room doors flew open.

Armed agents entered.

And at their head was William Royce.

He smiled slightly and looked straight at Rachel.

"That was a bold move. But don't forget, Miss Price..."

He took a step closer.

— The war is not over yet.

*****

Rachel felt the blood drain from her face as William Royce entered the conference room, surrounded by armed agents. There was no fear in his eyes. There was the pure, cold confidence of a man who believed he was still in control of the situation.

The journalists froze. The cameras were still recording.

Nathan, despite the pain, slowly stood up, looking straight into Royce's eyes.

"Mr. Royce," he said in an icy tone. "Have you come here to watch your end?"

Royce smiled slightly and slowly walked closer.

"My end?" he repeated, looking around the room. "Mr. Bishop, do you really think you can stop me?"

Rachel stepped forward, holding the papers in her hand.

— It's already happened. All the media have copies.

Royce looked at her with amusement.

— Do you really believe that one set of documents can destroy me?

Hayes stood up and walked closer.

— These documents are more than just a list of names. They are the scheme of how the system works, its financing, its contacts, the people you destroyed.

Royce looked at him contemptuously.

— And what are you going to do with it? Publish it?

Rachel lifted her chin.

— Yes. And that's why you're here.

Royce smiled wider.

— Ah … so you're not that naive after all.

Nathan frowned.

- What do you mean?

Royce turned to his men.

— Tell them.

The agent to his left took out a phone and pressed a few buttons.

An image appeared on the big screen in the conference room.

News station.

The presenter said something in a nervous voice.

— …According to sources close to the Justice Department, today's press conference regarding an alleged political scandal was a hoax. Evidence has emerged indicating that the documents were doctored by a group linked to foreign intelligence agencies…

Rachel felt her legs give way beneath her.

- NO…

Royce turned to them, triumphant.

— See? I've already won.

Nathan clenched his fists.

— Do you think people will believe you?

Royce raised his eyebrows.

— They don't have to believe me. It's enough that they doubt you.

Rachel glanced at the screens. The news was now showing doctored evidence, "intelligence reports" suggesting the documents they had released were the work of foreign agents.

Hayes frowned.

— When did you prepare it?

Royce shrugged.

— I always have a plan B.

Eleanor finally spoke up.

— If you think that one manipulated recording will save you, you are wrong.

Royce looked at her, a spark of something that might have been admiration in his eyes.

"Mrs. Price, please. You know better. I'm not acting alone."

Nathan looked at Rachel and Eleanor.

— We have to get out of here.

Royce heard this and smiled.

— I'll be happy to help you.

He waved his hand and his men moved aside, making way for them to the door.

— You can go. No one will stop you.

Rachel looked at him suspiciously.

— And you're just going to let us go?

Royce spread his hands.

"You're just desperate now. You've just been discredited in front of the whole world. You're the ones who are running away now."

Nathan looked at Rachel and Eleanor.

— Let's go.

They walked out slowly, knowing Royce was watching them.

As the door closed behind them, Rachel looked at Nathan.

— What now?

Nathan clenched his jaw.

— We will find a way.

Eleanor looked toward the city.

— And this time we have to strike harder.

*****

Nathan, Rachel, and Eleanor hid in a safe apartment that Holloway provided for them.

They sat in silence.

On TV and on the Internet, one topic dominated: disproving their credibility.

Rachel looked at Nathan.

— What if we can't win?

Nathan looked at her calmly.

"We can. But we have to find something Royce can't dispute."

Hayes entered the room carrying a laptop.

— I have something.

Everyone looked at him.

— Royce controls the media, controls the politicians. But there is one area he does not fully control.

Rachel narrowed her eyes.

- What?

Hayes smiled slightly.

— Intelligence services.

Nathan looked at the laptop screen.

- What do you mean?

Hayes turned the laptop toward them.

"I found traces of the CIA covert operations that Royce tried to clean up. Some of those documents survived in encrypted archives."

Rachel held her breath.

—You mean there are... copies somewhere?

Hayes nodded.

— Or, more precisely, in Langley.

Nathan looked at Rachel and Eleanor.

— If we get there…

Eleanor finished for him:

—We can take down Royce once and for all.

Rachel looked at Nathan.

— So we're hacking into CIA headquarters?

Nathan smiled slightly.

— Well… I guess I've always wanted to do it.

The plan was simple but risky.

Nathan, Rachel, and Eleanor were to infiltrate CIA headquarters in Langley, find hidden copies of Royce's documents, and release them to the world before Royce found them.

Holloway provided them with false passes and access to a hidden entrance.

Rachel looked at Nathan as they stood in front of the building.

"If Royce finds out we're here, there'll be no turning back."

Nathan took a deep breath.

- I know.

He looked at Eleanor.

— Ready?

Eleanor nodded.

— I've been running from this man for forty years. Today we end it once and for all.

Nathan smiled slightly.

— In that case, let's go in.

They stepped forward, passing through the front door.

Little did they know that Royce already knew where they were.

And that this time he had no intention of letting them go alive.

*****

Nathan, Rachel, and Eleanor walked through the front doors of the CIA building in Langley, trying to look like people who had every right to be there.

Holloway had gotten them fake IDs, but Nathan knew it was only a matter of time before the security systems started checking them.

Rachel looked at him worriedly.

— How much time do we have?

Nathan glanced at his watch.

— Maybe fifteen minutes. Maybe less.

Eleanor looked at the markings on the wall.

— The archives are on the fourth level.

Hayes, who was waiting in the car, spoke into the earpiece in Nathan's ear.

— You're in the system. The cameras haven't detected you, but that won't last long.

Nathan looked at Rachel.

— We have to hurry.

They walked down the corridor, past offices and agents who paid them no attention.

When they reached the elevator, Eleanor pressed the button.

"If Royce knows we're here, he could be watching us already."

Nathan looked at her.

- I know.

The elevator opened. They stepped inside and Nathan pressed the "-4" button.

The door closed.

Rachel took a deep breath.

— If this works, it will be the biggest scandal in the history of this country.

Nathan looked at her.

— If not, they won't even have time to bury us.

The elevator was going down.

And then the security system activated.

"ALARM. UNAUTHORIZED ACCESS. PROTECTION ON THE ROAD."

Rachel looked at Nathan with wide eyes.

— Shit…

Nathan immediately opened the elevator control panel and began manipulating the wires.

— Give me a few seconds!

Eleanor pressed herself against the wall.

— We don't have a few seconds!

Rachel glanced at the display.

The elevator stopped between floors.

Hayes shouted over the phone:

— Royce's men are already in the building!

Rachel looked at the control panel.

—Nathan, if you have some magical way to fix this, now is the time!

Nathan connected the two wires and the elevator started moving again.

— Hold on!

They descended to the fourth level.

The door hissed open.

Rachel jumped out first, Nathan after her. Eleanor followed last.

They were running towards the archives when suddenly a voice rang out from the end of the corridor:

— STOP!

Rachel looked to the side.

Two armed guards ran towards them.

Nathan pulled Rachel and Eleanor behind the bookshelf.

— The door to the archives is at the end of the hall. We have to get there.

Eleanor looked at Nathan.

— We have no weapons.

Nathan smiled slightly.

— Then we have to be faster.

Rachel ran first, heading for the archive door.

Nathan stopped and knocked over a bookshelf, blocking the guards' path.

— That'll buy us a few seconds!

Eleanor pressed a button on the panel next to the door.

"BIOMETRIC AUTHORIZATION REQUIRED."

Rachel looked at Nathan.

— And what now?!

Nathan glanced to the side and saw one of the scientists trying to escape.

He ran up to him and grabbed his arm.

— We need your access!

The man looked at him in horror.

— I don't know who you are, but…

Nathan pressed into his hand the thick envelope of cash that Holloway had given them just in case.

— Now you know.

The scientist looked at the money, then at Rachel.

He sighed and placed his hand on the reader.

"ACCESS APPROVED."

The door opened.

Nathan looked at the scientist.

— We were never here.

The man nodded and quickly walked away.

Rachel and Eleanor ran inside.

Nathan closed the door behind them and locked the system.

— We have a few minutes.

Rachel looked around the room.

hundreds of safes and hard drives inside.

Eleanor walked over to the terminal.

— We need to find Royce's files.

Rachel glanced at the keyboard.

— Anything specific?

Eleanor began typing in passwords she remembered from years ago.

—If Royce was part of the arrangement from the beginning, his name will be associated with the first operations.

Nathan looked at the screen.

— Try "Project Cyclope."

Eleanor typed in the name.

"LOADING DATA..."

Rachel held her breath.

top secret level files appeared on the screen .

Nathan looked at the headlines.

"SPECIAL OPERATIONS 1982-2024"
"FINANCING UNOFFICIAL PROGRAMS"
"ESTABLISHMENT OF THE TRADE"

Rachel looked at Eleanor.

— That's it.

Nathan plugged in the flash drive and started copying files.

Progress: 15%…

Hayes spoke on the phone.

"Royce's men are trying to get in! You've got three minutes max!"

Nathan looked at the screen.

Progress: 40%…

Eleanor watched the door nervously.

— If they find us here…

Rachel looked at Nathan.

— We'll end up like Calloway.

Nathan looked at the screen.

Progress: 85%…

Suddenly the lights in the room went out.

Rachel held her breath.

- What happened?!

Eleanor looked at the screen.

— Someone cut the power.

Nathan looked at the disk.

Progress: 98%…

Hayes shouted over the phone:

— They're opening the door!

Nathan pulled out a flash drive.

— We got it!

Rachel looked at the door as it began to open.

Five armed men stood in the doorway.

And at the end of the corridor…

William Royce.

He looked at them and smiled slightly.

— It's over, Mr. Bishop.

Nathan clenched his fists.

- Not yet.

*****

Nathan stared at William Royce, who stood in the archive doorway, surrounded by armed men. His face was calm, confident—as if he already knew he had won.

Rachel squeezed Eleanor's hand, and Nathan hid the flash drive in his inside jacket pocket.

"It's over, Mr. Bishop ," Royce repeated.

Nathan looked at him with a cold gaze.

— It's over for you.

Royce sighed and looked at his men.

— It's always the same. You try to fight, but you forget one thing...

He took a step forward.

— I always have a plan.

At that moment the lights in the building came back on and the security system speakers sounded a warning.

"SECURITY RESTORED. ONLINE SYSTEM."

Nathan glanced at Eleanor and Rachel. This was their only chance.

It's now or never.

*****

Nathan was the first to spring into action.

He grabbed a lamp from the desk and threw it straight at one of Royce's bodyguards.

Chaos reigned.

Rachel and Eleanor ran toward the side door that led to the utility corridor.

"This way! " Rachel shouted.

Nathan followed them, but Royce had no intention of letting them go.

— Stop them!

The security guards raised their weapons.

Nathan threw himself to the ground, pulling Rachel and Eleanor with him.

Shots rang out in the air.

The bullets hit the metal shelves, scattering documents across the room.

Nathan rose first, grabbing Eleanor by the arm and pulling her toward the door.

Rachel pulled out a small knife she had hidden in her pocket and lunged at the nearest guard, slashing him across the forearm.

The man screamed and dropped the gun.

Rachel kicked her further.

Nathan pulled out his gun, which he had taken from Holloway's safe earlier, and fired at the light, shattering the bulbs.

The twilight gave them an advantage.

"Run! " he shouted to Rachel and Eleanor.

Eleanor ran into the maintenance corridor first, with Rachel close behind.

Nathan looked at Royce one last time.

The man stood still, looking at him with icy confidence.

— Run all you want, Bishop. It doesn't matter.

Nathan didn't answer. He turned and ran.

They ran along the corridor that led to the underground garage.

Hayes spoke into their headphones.

— I have you on camera! Security is closing the exits!

Nathan looked at Eleanor.

— Will you find another way?

Eleanor glanced at the markings on the wall.

" There's a side exit leading to a ventilation shaft. If we get to it..."

" Bishop! You've got one second before they surround you! " Hayes warned.

Nathan decided.

— Let's run!

Rachel ran first, Eleanor close behind. Nathan covered their rear.

More footsteps were heard in the distance. Royce's men were getting closer.

Finally, they reached the side door.

Nathan kicked it hard.

Behind them was a narrow ventilation shaft leading to the rear of the building.

Rachel looked at Eleanor.

— You go in first!

Eleanor, despite her age, began to climb up the shaft.

Rachel followed her.

Nathan looked toward the hallway.

He knew this was their last chance to escape.

But Royce wasn't going to let them do that.

The door at the end of the corridor swung open.

Two of Royce's bodyguards rushed inside.

Nathan raised his gun and fired.

He hit the first one in the shoulder.

The second one rushed towards him.

Nathan didn't have time to raise his weapon, so he did the only thing he could.

He punched him right in the face.

The man staggered.

Nathan took advantage of the moment, kicked him in the stomach and rushed toward the shaft.

Rachel shook his hand.

— Nathan, hurry up!

Nathan grabbed the metal edges and stepped inside.

Another shot rang out right behind him.

The bullet stopped on the metal casing of the shaft.

Nathan looked down.

They were safe.

For now…

*****

After a few minutes they reached the exit on the other side of the building.

Eleanor went outside first, then Rachel.

Nathan looked at his phone and called Hayes.

— We got this. We gotta get out of here.

Hayes nodded.

— The car is waiting around the corner. But we have a problem.

Rachel looked at Nathan.

- What?

Hayes took a deep breath.

—Royce declared you to be terrorists.

Nathan froze.

- What?!

Hayes put the speaker on.

A reporter's voice came from the radio:

— "Nathan Bishop, Rachel Price and Eleanor Price are wanted by the U.S. government. According to CIA-linked sources, they were part of a plot to destabilize the country."

Rachel felt her hands begin to tremble.

— He has already started the counterattack.

Nathan looked at Eleanor.

— We have to disappear. Now.

Hayes started the engine.

" I've got one place we can hide. But if Royce finds us, it's over."

Nathan looked toward the city.

He knew this was their last chance.

And that Royce wasn't finished yet.

They were now being hunted.

Royce had the FBI, CIA and the media on his side.

Nathan, Rachel, and Eleanor only had each other…

And one flash drive that could destroy an entire empire of power.

Nathan looked at Rachel.

— Now we are the system.

Rachel looked into his eyes.

—So it's time to show Royce what that means.

*****

Nathan, Rachel, and Eleanor raced through the narrow streets of suburban Virginia in a black SUV driven by Hayes.

Every streetlight we passed seemed suspicious. Every car could have been another Fed vehicle.

Rachel glanced in the side mirror.

— I don't see them.

Nathan, sitting next to Hayes, checked his phone.

— This is the calm before the storm. Royce won't let up.

Hayes turned onto a side road that led deeper into the forest.

— I have a safe place for a few hours. Then we have to get out.

Rachel looked at him suspiciously.

- Where?

Hayes smiled slightly.

— To the only man who can help us.

Nathan looked at him.

— Who do you mean?

Hayes took a deep breath.

—FBI Director Robert Kingsley.

*****

A few hours later they were in an old house in the middle of nowhere.

Nathan sat at the table, analyzing files on a flash drive.

Rachel looked at him.

— Do you have anything?

Nathan rubbed his face with his hands.

— Yes. But if what's here is real, then Royce isn't the only problem.

Eleanor stepped closer.

- What do you mean?

Nathan looked up.

— Royce did not act alone.

Rachel frowned.

— We knew it from the beginning.

Nathan shook his head.

"You don't understand. I have transactions here that lead to people in the Pentagon, the White House, even..."

He stopped.

Rachel leaned forward.

—Nathan, what?

Nathan took a deep breath.

—CIA .

There was silence.

Eleanor leaned against the wall.

— It's impossible…

Hayes looked at them.

"If the CIA was involved, Royce has more people than we thought. "

Nathan looked at Eleanor.

— It wasn't a deal. It was a state within a state.

Rachel looked at the flash drive.

— So who's in charge now?

Nathan sighed.

— Royce. But not alone.

Eleanor clenched her fists.

— So we have to break up this whole empire.

Hayes checked his watch.

" Kingsley will be waiting in two hours. We need to get moving."

Rachel looked at Nathan.

— Are you sure we can trust him?

Nathan didn't respond immediately.

Finally, he looked her in the eye.

- NO.

The FBI building in Washington looked like a fortress.

Nathan and Rachel sat in their car parked a few blocks away, watching the traffic on the street.

"If Royce knows we're here, it's an ambush," Rachel said.

Nathan looked at Eleanor and Hayes.

— Do you have a backup plan?

Hayes nodded.

"If you don't leave in an hour, Eleanor and I will contact the media."

Nathan took a deep breath.

- All right.

They got out of the car and walked to the entrance.

The receptionist looked at them suspiciously.

— Do you have an appointment?

—Nathan Bishop and Rachel Price. We're here to meet with Principal Kingsley.

The woman looked at them carefully, then picked up the phone and whispered something.

A few seconds later the office door opened.

Nathan and Rachel went inside.

Robert Kingsley sat behind the desk.

He looked at them with a cold gaze.

— I know why you're here.

Rachel and Nathan sat down across from Kingsley.

"Tell me something," Kingsley said, lacing his fingers together. "Why do you think I can help you?"

Nathan placed the flash drive on the desk.

—Because if Royce wins, you're next.

Kingsley smiled slightly.

— That's an interesting theory.

Rachel looked into his eyes.

— It's not a theory. It's a fact.

Kingsley took the flash drive and inserted it into his laptop.

A few minutes later his face hardened.

— Where did you get this?

Nathan replied quietly:

—Calloway.

Kingsley looked at them carefully.

—Royce will never let you reveal this.

Rachel straightened up.

— So you will help us?

Kingsley closed his laptop.

— I have to think about it.

Nathan narrowed his eyes.

— We don't have time.

Kingsley looked at him.

- I know.

Then the office door burst open.

Three FBI agents entered.

Armed.

Rachel held her breath.

Kingsley stood up slowly.

— I'm sorry, Mr. Bishop.

Nathan narrowed his eyes.

— You are with them.

Kingsley smiled slightly.

— I always have been.

*****

Rachel and Nathan were handcuffed and led out of the FBI building.

was waiting outside.

The door opened.

Inside sat William Royce.

He smiled.

— Get in.

Nathan looked at Rachel.

— This doesn't look good.

Rachel took a deep breath.

— It can't get any worse.

Royce laughed.

— Oh, believe me… maybe.

The limousine doors closed.

The car started moving.

Underground parking.

Nathan and Rachel were pulled from the car and led to a small, dark room.

Royce followed them in, closing the door.

He looked at them contemptuously.

— Did you really think you could stop me?

Nathan smiled slightly, despite the handcuffs.

— We'll stop you anyway.

Royce stepped closer and leaned into his ear.

—No, Mr. Bishop. You won't stop me. Because this time…

You won't get out of here alive.

*****

Nathan and Rachel sat in a dark concrete room, handcuffed to metal chairs. The fluorescent light flickered, casting cold, dead reflections on the walls.

Royce stood across the room, hands tucked into the pockets of his elegant coat. Beside him were two bodyguards—tall, well-built, faces devoid of emotion.

"I've always appreciated men who fight to the end," Royce said, slowly approaching. "But there's one thing you don't understand."

He looked at Nathan.

— You can't beat someone who has already won.

Nathan remained silent. He was not the type to respond to empty boasting.

Rachel looked at Royce with contempt.

— You haven't won yet.

Royce smiled slightly.

- NO?

He waved his hand and one of the security guards took out his phone and handed it to him.

— Let me show you what power looks like.

He raised the phone to his ear.

— Do it.

Nathan looked at Rachel.

The door opened and Robert Kingsley walked in.

Nathan clenched his jaw.

— I should have known.

Kingsley sat on the metal chair across from them and looked at Nathan with cool calm.

— You should.

Rachel leaned back in her chair.

— Why? What did Royce promise you?

Kingsley smiled slightly.

—Royce didn't promise me anything. He just won.

Nathan looked at Royce.

— So what now? Are you going to kill us?

Royce burst out laughing.

— Mr. Bishop, this isn't an action movie. I don't have to kill you.

He leaned closer.

— All I have to do is make you disappear.

*****

Eleanor sat in her hidden hideout in Virginia, nervously tapping her fingers on the table.

Hayes stood nearby, looking at the laptop.

— They should have contacted me a long time ago.

Eleanor looked at him.

— Royce has them.

Hayes nodded.

— So we need to act now.

He opened his laptop and entered the access code.

" I have something Royce didn't have time to remove."

Eleanor stepped closer.

- What is this?

An old recording appeared on the screen.

Royce sat in a dark room, talking to a man whose face could not be seen.

— "Kingsley is our trump card. If someone starts messing around, he'll shut it down."

Eleanor looked at Hayes.

— Is that enough?

Hayes smiled slightly.

— This is proof that the FBI is involved.

Eleanor looked at him seriously.

— So let's make use of it.

*****

Nathan heard Royce's phone vibrate faintly.

The man looked at the screen and his face instantly changed.

Kingsley noticed it first.

- What happened?

Royce stared at the phone.

— What the hell…

Nathan and Rachel exchanged a look.

Rachel raised an eyebrow.

— Did something go wrong?

Royce looked at them, but this time there was no confidence in his eyes.

Nathan leaned forward slightly.

— Something is happening.

Royce put the phone to his ear.

- What happened?!

Raised voices could be heard on the other end.

— Royce's tape just made it to CNN, the Washington Post, and several senators!

Royce looked at Kingsley.

— It's not possible!

Nathan smiled slightly.

— This is why you should always have a plan B.

Royce suddenly walked up to him and punched him in the face.

Nathan staggered but kept his eyes on Royce.

— It hurts, doesn't it?

Royce took a deep breath and looked at Kingsley.

— Lock them up. Forever.

Kingsley nodded and took a step toward the door.

But then…

The lights went out.

There was a bang.

And the door opened.

stood in the middle.

With a gun in his hand.

Royce turned around sharply, but Eleanor was already aiming the gun at him.

— Put your hands up.

Kingsley stepped back slowly.

Nathan looked at Eleanor.

— It took you a long time.

Eleanor smiled slightly.

— I had to make a spectacular entrance.

Rachel quickly freed herself from the handcuffs and reached for the guard's gun.

Hayes entered the room with a second gun.

"The whole country knows, Royce."

Royce looked at them and suddenly laughed.

— Do you really think this will be enough?

Nathan looked at Eleanor.

— Do we look like people who only think?

Royce took a step back.

Then the door opened a second time.

Five armed FBI agents entered.

Nathan and Rachel immediately raised their weapons.

But then one of the agents said in a cold tone:

—William Royce, you are under arrest for treason.

Rachel looked at Nathan.

— Did we just win?

Nathan looked at Royce, who was being handcuffed by the agents.

- I think so.

Royce looked at Kingsley.

— Do something!

Kingsley smiled slightly.

— I don't work for you anymore.

Rachel looked at Eleanor.

— What now?

Eleanor smiled slightly.

— Now we are fixing this country.

Nathan looked at Royce as the agents led him away.

—And you, Mr. Royce… you will have plenty of time to think about your mistakes.

Royce gave them a cold look.

— It's not over yet.

Nathan smiled slightly.

— For you? Yes, sir.

The door closed behind Royce.

Nathan took a deep breath.

Rachel looked at Eleanor.

— So, it's over?

Eleanor looked at her seriously.

— I'm afraid this is only the beginning...

*****

Within hours, news of Royce's arrest spread across the country.

The headlines screamed:

"WILLIAM ROYCE ARRESTED – HUGE POLITICAL SCANDAL"

"FORMER PRESIDENTIAL CANDIDATE ACCUSED OF CORRUPTION AND TRAUMA"

Nathan, Rachel, and Eleanor watched this in the hidden apartment.

Rachel looked at the screen.

— I can't believe this is actually happening.

Nathan sighed.

— It's not over yet.

Hayes turned away from the laptop.

— He's right. The FBI has officially taken over the investigation, but... something doesn't seem right.

Eleanor looked at him.

- What do you mean?

Hayes swiped his finger across the screen.

—Royce was arrested, but his men… weren't.

Nathan narrowed his eyes.

- That is?

Hayes took a deep breath.

— The system is still working.

Rachel looked at Nathan.

—That means Royce wasn't the only head of the snake.

Nathan placed his hands on the table.

— It means the war is just beginning.

*****

Four days later, Royce was still in federal custody, awaiting formal charges.

But one evening… he disappeared.

Rachel looked at the messages.

— Is this some kind of joke?!

Nathan put the phone down.

— No, it's a warning.

Eleanor clenched her fists.

— He shouldn't have disappeared.

Hayes looked at them.

— He didn't disappear. He was released.

Nathan looked at Rachel.

— The system is still alive.

Rachel swallowed hard.

— That means Royce will be back in the game.

Nathan clenched his jaw.

— And we have to be ready.

*****

Nathan Bishop stood in the dark room, staring at the television screen. William Royce, the man who had been in handcuffs just days before, was free again.

The headline at the bottom of the screen said it all:

"FBI CONFIRMS - ROYCE DISAPPEARED FROM COURT. NO TRACE OF BURGLARY."

Rachel sat on the couch, staring at the screen in disbelief.

— How is that possible?

Eleanor entered the room, holding a cup of coffee, and looked at them coldly.

— It's not impossible. It's a deal.

Hayes came in with his laptop and sat down next to Rachel.

" I checked. There's no record of Royce leaving the building. No recordings, no transaction. Officially, he should still be in his cell."

Nathan looked at Rachel.

— Someone high up helped him.

Rachel nodded.

— And that means we still have someone on the other side pulling the strings.

Eleanor looked at Nathan.

— So, who runs the system now?

Hayes took a deep breath.

— I think it's time to find out who really stands at the top of this pyramid.

Nathan and Rachel sat down to work through the documents they had managed to collect during the investigation.

"We know Royce had people in the FBI, the CIA, even the White House, " Rachel said. "But someone must have given him the order to run."

Nathan looked at the list of names.

—Royce was a pawn. A strong one, but still a pawn. Someone else is playing that game.

Eleanor looked at the documents.

— The system would not have worked for decades if it had not had more than political power.

Hayes looked up from his laptop.

— Money.

Rachel looked at him.

- What do you mean?

Hayes turned the screen towards them.

" I found something in Royce's files. The arrangement has ties to one of the largest investment funds in the world."

Nathan looked at the company name on the screen.

—Vanguard International.

Eleanor raised her eyebrows.

— They control billions of dollars.

Hayes nodded.

— Exactly. And it seems their president, a certain Alexander Wren, is more than just a financier.

Rachel frowned.

—So Royce was the public face of the system, but the real power always lay somewhere else.

Nathan looked at Eleanor.

— Time to visit Mr. Wren.

*****

Vanguard International had its headquarters in New York, in one of the tallest office buildings in Manhattan.

Nathan and Rachel stood in the lobby of the building, watching people in suits walk by.

"Do you think they'll let us just walk here? " Rachel asked.

Nathan smiled slightly.

— No. But that's why we have a plan.

They entered the building and approached the reception desk.

— Good morning. We have a meeting with Mr. Wren.

The receptionist looked at them suspiciously.

— Names?

Nathan smiled.

-Nathan Bishop and Rachel Price.

The woman looked at the monitor.

— There are no gentlemen on the list.

Rachel leaned over the counter.

— Please tell Mr. Wren we have information about William Royce.

The receptionist looked at them carefully, then reached for the phone.

A few seconds later she looked at them again.

— Mr. Wren can meet with you.

Nathan looked at Rachel.

— It was too easy.

Rachel nodded.

— That means he wants to talk to us too.

*****

Alexander Wren's office was on the top floor of the building.

They entered a spacious office overlooking the city.

Behind the desk sat a man in an elegant navy-blue suit, with graying hair and a cold gaze.

"Mr. Bishop, Miss Price ," he said, rising and extending his hand to them. "I've heard of you."

Nathan shook his hand.

— I'm glad you know who we are.

Wren smiled slightly and showed them to their seats.

— I assume you've come to talk about Royce.

Rachel sat down.

" This isn't a conversation. This is a warning. We know you and your company are connected to the system."

Wren adjusted his shirt cuffs.

— The arrangement. Is that what you call it?

Nathan looked at him carefully.

— What do you call him?

Wren smiled slightly.

— Business.

Rachel clenched her hands.

— Royce has fallen. The system is beginning to fall apart. It's over.

Wren leaned forward slightly.

—Miss Price, listen to me very carefully.

His voice became soft, almost hypnotizing.

" The system didn't fail. Royce was just one of many. What you did was spectacular, but it doesn't change anything."

Nathan looked at him with a cold gaze.

— We're not here for a lecture. We're here for the truth.

Wren looked him in the eye.

— So maybe let's talk about the truth.

Rachel felt a cold shiver run down her spine.

— What do you mean?

Wren leaned back in his chair and folded his hands.

" The truth is that Royce didn't act alone. And now... you're the target."

Nathan looked at Rachel.

— Did we just fall into another trap?

Wren smiled.

— I'd rather say you just opened a door you shouldn't have opened.

Nathan looked at Alexander Wren, trying to judge how much truth there was in his words.

"What are you suggesting?" he asked coldly.

Wren smiled slightly.

— I suggest you are fighting something you do not understand.

Rachel laced her fingers under the table, trying to hide her nervousness.

— We know more than you think.

Wren nodded.

- Really?

He looked at them with curiosity and opened the laptop standing on the desk.

After a moment, the screen lit up with a series of photos and documents.

Rachel held her breath.

Pictures of themselves.

Nathan, Rachel, Eleanor, Hayes. Every step, every trip, every conversation over the past few months.

Nathan clenched his fists.

— How long have you been following us?

Wren leaned back in his chair.

— From day one.

Rachel looked at Nathan, then back at the screen.

— What do you want?

Wren closed his laptop and looked at them seriously.

— I want you to stop.

Nathan burst out laughing.

— After all this, do you really think we'll back down?

Wren sighed as if talking to a stubborn child.

— I'm not asking you to do this. I'm saying it's the only way to survive.

Rachel leaned forward slightly.

— And if we refuse?

Wren smiled slightly.

— Royce will be the least of your problems.

Nathan glanced at Rachel and Eleanor.

— Who else is involved in this?

Wren looked at them seriously.

" Royce was one of us once. But he got too ambitious. An arrangement isn't one man, Mr. Bishop. It's a system."

Rachel narrowed her eyes.

— So, who's in charge now?

Wren didn't respond immediately.

He reached into his desk drawer, pulled out an envelope, and placed it in front of Nathan.

— If you want to survive, leave. Now.

Nathan picked up the envelope and looked inside.

Fake passports. Flight tickets to Europe.

Rachel shook her head.

— Do you think we will let ourselves be bought?

Wren looked at her with something that might have been a shadow of respect.

— No. But I'm giving you a chance.

Nathan stood up and placed his hands on the desk.

— We won't run away.

Wren sighed and closed his laptop.

— So you just signed your own death warrant.

*****

Nathan and Rachel left Wren's office and headed for the elevator.

"Was that a threat?" Rachel asked.

Nathan nodded.

— Yes. But not only that.

Rachel looked at him.

- What do you mean?

Nathan squeezed the envelope in his hand.

" He wasn't just trying to scare us. He really thinks we're dead."

Rachel swallowed hard.

— So, what now?

Nathan looked at her seriously.

—Now we need to find out who Wren really is and who he works for.

The elevator stopped on the ground floor, and they stepped out onto the streets of New York.

At that same moment Rachel felt a strange twinge in the back of her neck.

Nathan looked at her.

— What is it?

Rachel glanced at the building behind them.

— We have a tail.

Nathan clenched his jaw.

— Okay. We're splitting up.

Rachel and Nathan got separated in the crowd.

Nathan turned into a side street and quickened his pace.

Rachel went the other way, weaving through the people.

After a few minutes she reached the cafe and went inside.

It was too quiet.

She glanced out the window.

A black sedan was parked across the street.

Rachel sat down at the table and took out her phone.

She sent a quick message to Nathan.

"We have a problem."

The reply came a few seconds later.

"Don't move. Is anyone inside?"

Rachel glanced at the entrance.

"Not yet."

And then the cafe door opened.

A man in an elegant suit entered and looked straight at her.

Rachel closed her eyes for a second and took a deep breath.

She opened them and looked him straight in the face.

— I knew you would find me.

The man smiled slightly.

— Long time no see, Rachel.

Nathan wrote another text message.

"Who is he?"

Rachel looked at the man in front of her.

— What do you want, Ethan?

Nathan received the message.

"Ethan Cole."

Nathan felt his heart start beating faster.

Cole was a former CIA agent.

And a man who once worked for Royce.

*****

Rachel looked at Ethan Cole. He still had the same cool smile she remembered from years ago. He had been one of the CIA's best agents before he dropped off the radar.

—You didn't look surprised, Rachel.

Rachel leaned back in her chair.

— Because I'm not.

Ethan sat down across from her and spread his arms.

— Good. Because we need to talk.

Rachel narrowed her eyes.

— About what?

Ethan looked at her carefully.

— That you just got yourself into something you don't understand.

Rachel felt her phone vibrate in her pocket.

Nathan: "On his way. Keep him busy."

She looked at Ethan and raised an eyebrow.

" I don't understand? I thought Royce was the head of the system."

Ethan smiled slightly.

" Royce? He was just a tool. And now that he's gone, someone has to take his place."

Rachel swallowed hard.

— Wren.

Ethan nodded.

— Wren. And a few others.

Rachel looked into his eyes.

— And you too, right?

Ethan looked at her without emotion.

— I'm not here to threaten you. I'm here to give you a choice.

Rachel leaned forward.

— What choice?

Ethan smiled slightly.

— You either disappear or end up dead.

*****

Nathan entered the cafe through the side entrance and sat down a few tables away.

Seeing Ethan Cole, he felt a familiar knot in his stomach.

If he is here, it means things are more serious than we thought.

Rachel kept a straight face.

— Is this an offer? I'll back out and you'll leave me alone?

Ethan nodded.

" Not just you. Your mother. Bishop. Hayes. You can start over."

Rachel looked at him carefully.

— And if I refuse?

Ethan sighed and took a sip of coffee.

— If you refuse, you'll be dead within a week.

Nathan looked at Ethan, assessing the situation.

If he wants us to retreat, it means we still have the upper hand.

Rachel leaned forward.

— What if I say I want something in return?

Ethan raised his eyebrows.

- I'm listening.

Rachel smiled slightly.

— I want Royce.

Ethan was silent for a moment, then shook his head.

— I can't give it to you.

Rachel looked at him carefully.

— Because he's still part of the deal, right?

Ethan did not respond.

Nathan stood up and walked closer.

— So Royce is alive. And he still has influence.

Ethan looked at him with a slight smile.

—I knew you were here somewhere, Bishop.

Nathan sat down next to Rachel and looked him straight in the eye.

— Tell us where Royce is.

Ethan looked at them calmly.

- I can't.

Rachel narrowed her eyes.

— Are you afraid of him?

Ethan smiled slightly.

— I'm not afraid of anyone. But if you think Royce is your biggest problem, you're wrong.

Nathan leaned forward.

— So, who is it?

Ethan looked at them and stood up.

— Find out for yourself.

He turned around and headed for the exit.

Rachel looked at Nathan.

— What now?

Nathan clenched his fists.

— We find Royce.

*****

Two hours later they were sitting in a secret apartment in Washington.

Hayes scrolled through documents on his laptop.

— Royce was last seen at a military base in Nevada. Then the trail goes cold.

Eleanor looked at the screen.

— If they're hiding him at a military base, it means he has stronger connections than we thought.

Nathan looked at Rachel.

— We have to find him.

Rachel nodded.

— How much time do we have?

Hayes glanced at his watch.

— We don't know when he'll reappear. But one thing's for sure.

Nathan looked at him.

- What?

Hayes closed his laptop.

— Royce isn't hiding. He's preparing.

The system was still working.

Royce was alive.

And if he had access to a military base, that means he was planning something bigger.

Nathan and Rachel knew one thing:

That wasn't the end of the story yet.

Eleanor looked at them.

— So what do we do?

Nathan looked at her with a cold smile.

— We find him first.

Rachel looked at Nathan.

— And this time we're finishing him off.

*****

Nathan, Rachel, and Hayes left Washington and headed toward Nevada.

They didn't know what they would find.

But they knew one thing:

Royce wasn't going to wait for them to get to him.

The arrangement has changed.

Now Royce had power he had never had before.

And if they don't stop him in time...

The whole country will pay the price.

*****

A black SUV sped down a Nevada desert road, raising a cloud of dust behind it.

Nathan was driving, Rachel was sitting next to him, and Hayes was in the backseat checking data on his laptop.

" We're less than an hour away from where I believe Royce was last seen."

Rachel looked at Nathan.

— Military base?

Hayes nodded.

— Theoretically closed for years. But there are signals that it's just a cover.

Nathan looked at the road ahead of them.

" If Royce is there, it won't be easy."

Rachel glanced at the GPS.

— What do we know about this place?

Hayes moved some files around on the screen.

— Officially, Lockwood Base was closed in 2009. Unofficially, it has been used for intelligence operations for years. Royce had contacts there even before he became a senator.

Nathan gripped the steering wheel.

— And now it's there again.

Rachel looked at Nathan.

— So what do we do?

Nathan looked at her seriously.

— We're going in there. But we can't make a mistake.

Hayes closed his laptop and leaned back in his seat.

" If Royce has protection there, we'll have to act fast."

Rachel looked out the window at the desert plain.

— This looks like the end of the world.

Nathan smiled slightly.

— Maybe this is the end of the world.

Nathan stopped the car half a mile from the base.

— We continue on foot.

Rachel and Hayes got out, and Nathan opened the trunk and pulled out his backpack with his gear.

— Cameras, night vision goggles, burglary kit.

Hayes looked at the buildings in the distance.

— It doesn't look abandoned.

Rachel narrowed her eyes.

- Is not.

Nathan looked at her.

— What do you see?

Rachel pointed to the fence surrounding the base.

— Cameras are working. Motion sensors. And guards.

Hayes looked through the binoculars.

— And these aren't just security guards. These are mercenaries.

Nathan nodded.

— Royce doesn't trust anyone in the government.

Rachel turned to Nathan.

— So how do we get there?

Nathan looked at Hayes.

— Do you have something for us?

Hayes smiled and opened his laptop.

— I can give you five minutes without cameras. The rest is up to you.

Nathan looked at Rachel.

— That's enough for us.

They crawled in the dark along the base fence.

Hayes counted down into the receiver.

— You have thirty seconds until the cameras turn off.

Rachel looked at Nathan.

— Are you ready?

Nathan took a metal cutter out of his backpack.

- Always.

Hayes counted down:

— Three… two… one… cameras offline.

Nathan started cutting the fence.

Rachel stayed awake, listening.

After a while they opened the passage and crawled through to the other side.

Nathan looked at the hangars in the distance.

— If Royce is here, that's where we'll find him.

Rachel checked her watch.

— We have five minutes before the system comes back on.

Nathan nodded.

— Let's not waste them.

*****

The base was quiet, but Nathan knew it was an illusion.

Rachel walked over to the hangar door and tried to open it.

— Closed.

Nathan took out the lockpicks.

— Not for long.

After a moment the door opened.

They went inside.

And then they saw something they didn't expect.

Plane.

Freshly fueled, ready to fly.

Rachel looked at Nathan.

— Royce is running away.

Hayes spoke on the phone.

— Nathan, we have a problem.

Nathan clenched his jaw.

- What's going on?

Hayes took a deep breath.

— The cameras are back. They know you're here.

At that same moment an alarm sounded in the hangar.

Rachel looked at Nathan.

— Time to get out of here.

Nathan looked at the plane.

— No. Time to get Royce.

Royce stood at the end of the hangar, flanked by two bodyguards.

He looked at Nathan and Rachel and smiled slightly.

— I knew you would find me.

Nathan raised his gun.

— Get out of my way, Royce.

Royce laughed.

— So what will you do? Will you shoot me?

Rachel looked at the security guards.

— It will end today.

Royce took a step closer.

—No , Rachel. This is just beginning.

At that moment the security guards raised their weapons.

Nathan and Rachel dived behind the crates as the first shots rang out.

Hayes shouted into the phone.

— You've got the whole fucking army on your back! Get out of there!

Rachel looked at Nathan.

— What are we doing?!

Nathan looked at Royce.

— We won't let him escape.

Shots echoed through the hangar.

Nathan and Rachel hid behind crates while Royce's bodyguards fired at them.

Rachel looked at Nathan.

" We can't get stuck here! If Royce gets on that plane, we'll lose him forever!"

Nathan looked toward the plane. Royce was walking toward him, flanked by two bodyguards.

— We have to cut him off.

Rachel glanced at the fuel crates.

— I have an idea.

She raised the gun, aimed it at one of the crates, and pulled the trigger.

The shell hit the fuel tank, which spilled onto the concrete floor.

Nathan understood her plan.

— If we cut him off from the plane…

Rachel smiled slightly.

— Then he won't have anywhere to escape.

*****

Royce stopped when he saw the spilled fuel.

The security guards stopped shooting.

Nathan stood up from behind the crates, holding the gun.

— It's over, Royce.

Royce looked at him mockingly.

— Really? Because all I see are two people who are about to die.

He raised his hand, signaling to his men.

Rachel looked at Nathan.

— Do you still have that fuse?

Nathan took a small lighter out of his pocket.

— You mean this?

Royce looked at them, then burst out laughing.

— You don't have the courage.

Nathan smiled slightly.

- NO?

And then he threw the lighter right into the spilled fuel.

The fire exploded in a second, creating a wall of flames between Royce and the plane.

The security guards jumped back.

Royce looked at the flames in horror.

— What the hell...?!

Nathan stepped closer, aiming the gun at him.

— Now you have nowhere to run.

Rachel held him at gunpoint.

— Surrender, Royce. It's over.

Royce looked at them furiously.

— Do you really think this is the end?

At that moment they heard sirens.

Rachel glanced at Nathan.

- What is this?

Nathan glanced at the hangar door.

— Problems.

The hangar doors opened with a bang.

A dozen or so people in black uniforms ran inside.

Rachel frowned.

— This isn't the FBI...

Nathan looked at Royce.

— Who are they?

Royce smiled slightly.

— My new friends.

The man at the head of the group took out his ID badge.

— Major Scott Harrison, Special Forces.

Nathan narrowed his eyes.

— What is the army doing here?

Harrison looked at Royce.

— We're taking our man.

Rachel took a step forward.

— Royce is a traitor. He is wanted.

Harrison smiled slightly.

— Not by us.

Nathan looked at Royce.

— So you work for the military now?

Royce adjusted the cuffs of his suit.

— I've always worked.

Rachel looked at Nathan.

— This is bigger than we thought.

Nathan gripped the gun.

— And that's why we can't let him go.

Major Harrison looked at Nathan.

— Please put down your weapon.

Nathan didn't move.

— I won't let you take him.

Harrison sighed and looked at his men.

— If you don't put your weapons down, we will shoot you.

Rachel looked at Nathan.

— We can't win this fight.

Nathan clenched his jaw.

He looked at Royce.

— It's not over yet.

Royce smiled slightly.

— Yes, Mr. Bishop. It's over now.

Harrison nodded as his men surrounded Royce and led him out of the hangar.

Rachel looked at Nathan.

— What now?

Nathan watched Royce board the military helicopter.

— Now we'll find out who's really pulling the strings.

Nathan and Rachel returned to the hidden apartment where Eleanor and Hayes were waiting for them.

Hayes looked at their faces.

— You lost Royce, didn't you?

Rachel sat down on the couch.

— The army took him away.

Eleanor frowned.

- Army?

Nathan nodded.

— This wasn't just a conspiracy. This was a military operation.

Hayes looked at the laptop.

— Which means Royce is not our only problem.

Nathan looked at Rachel.

— We need to find out who Major Harrison really is.

Rachel took a deep breath.

—And why the army is protecting Royce.

Eleanor looked at them seriously.

— So now we're not just fighting politicians.

Nathan nodded.

— Now we are fighting the entire system.

*****

Nathan sat at the table, staring at his laptop while Hayes scrolled through pages of encrypted files.

Rachel stood by the window, looking out onto the street. They still had a few hours before anyone would come looking for them, but she knew it wouldn't be long.

Eleanor poured herself some coffee and looked at the screen.

— Do we have anything on this Harrison?

Hayes shook his head.

" Nothing official. But I found reports of covert operations in Afghanistan and Syria. All conducted by people who now work for Royce."

Nathan looked at the list of names.

— So the military was involved from the very beginning.

Rachel walked over to the table.

— We need to know who Harrison really is.

Hayes clicked a few times and a report from years ago appeared on the screen.

— Here's something interesting.

Nathan leaned closer.

"OPERATION SCARLET. 2010. CLASSIFICATION: TOP SECRET."

Rachel looked at the title of the document.

- What is this?

Hayes opened the file.

" This is an operation that Harrison ran in Iraq. They were sending weapons to paramilitary groups. And guess who was funding the whole project?"

Nathan looked at Rachel.

—Vanguard International.

Eleanor took a deep breath.

— That's Alexander Wren.

Rachel rubbed her face with her hands.

— So now we have connections between politics, the military and big business.

Nathan looked at the screen.

— This is no longer a conspiracy. This is a government in the shadows.

Rachel closed her laptop.

— We have to find Harrison.

Hayes shook his head.

— It won't be that simple.

Nathan looked at him.

— Everyone has a weak spot. Find it for me.

Hayes opened a new page and started searching.

— Okay. We have some private accounts that don't match his official income.

Eleanor looked at the screen.

— So he's corrupt.

Rachel looked at Nathan.

— We can push him.

Nathan nodded.

— This is our only option.

*****

Twenty-four hours later, Nathan and Rachel were sitting in a black van parked in front of a luxury apartment building in Arlington.

Hayes spoke into the receiver.

" Harrison just got home. You have five minutes before his security changes."

Nathan looked at Rachel.

— Ready?

Rachel smiled slightly.

- Always.

They got out of the van and walked towards the building.

Nathan and Rachel walked up to the door of Harrison's apartment.

Rachel looked at Nathan.

— Should we knock or force our way in?

Nathan took out the skeleton key.

— Let's not waste time.

After a few seconds the door opened.

Harrison was sitting on the couch, drinking whiskey.

When he saw them enter, he narrowed his eyes.

— I knew very well that you would come.

Nathan closed the door behind him.

— So you know why we're here.

Harrison put down his glass and looked at them with a cold smile.

— You've got balls to come here.

Rachel stepped closer.

— We have something that could destroy you.

Harrison raised his eyebrows.

- Really?

Nathan threw a stack of papers on the table for him.

" We know your connections to Wren and Royce. We know about Operation Scarlet. We know you were a key player in the arrangement."

Harrison looked at the documents and smiled.

— You are playing a dangerous game.

Rachel looked at him coldly.

— We can say the same about you.

Harrison took a sip of whiskey and looked at them.

— What do you want?

Nathan sat down across from him.

— Where's Royce?

Harrison looked at him for a moment, then sighed and shook his head.

— You're so damn stubborn.

Rachel leaned over the table.

— Where. He. Is.

Harrison looked into her eyes.

— In Mexico.

Nathan narrowed his eyes.

— Mexico?

Harrison nodded.

" The system has a safe haven there. If Royce is there, it's because he's planning something bigger."

Rachel looked at Nathan.

— We have to find him.

Harrison stood up and poured himself another glass of whiskey.

— If you are going there, I have some advice for you.

Nathan looked at him.

- What?

Harrison smiled slightly.

— Before you show up, prepare your will.

*****

Four hours later Nathan, Rachel, and Hayes were on a private plane bound for Mexico.

Rachel looked at Nathan.

— You didn't look convinced.

Nathan looked out the window.

— Because something is not right here.

Hayes looked at them from his laptop.

— Do you think it's a trap?

Nathan took a deep breath.

— I know it's a trap.

Rachel leaned back in her chair.

— So why are we flying straight into it?

Nathan looked at her seriously.

" Because if Royce is really out there, this might be our only chance to end this."

Eleanor looked at them.

— And if this is our only chance, then we have to be ready.

Nathan looked at Rachel.

— Are you ready?

Rachel smiled slightly.

- Always.

Nathan looked at his phone screen, which showed a message from Harrison.

"If you find him, know this - Royce never acted alone."

Nathan looked at Rachel and Eleanor.

— It's not over yet.

The plane shook slightly and a message appeared on the screen.

"We're approaching Mexico."

Nathan took a deep breath.

— This is just the beginning.

*****

The plane landed at a small, private airport on the outskirts of Mexico.

Rachel looked at Nathan.

— Do you have any contacts here?

Nathan took out his phone and scrolled through the list of numbers.

— There is one person. But I haven't seen her for years.

Hayes closed his laptop.

— Who is that?

Nathan looked at him.

—Miguel Alvarez.

Eleanor looked at Nathan carefully.

— Is this the same Alvarez who used to work for the DEA?

Nathan nodded.

— Now he works for himself.

Rachel crossed her arms.

— Can we trust him?

Nathan smiled slightly.

— No. But he's the only man who can help us find Royce.

Forty minutes later they were driving on back roads toward an old ranch on the outskirts of town.

Rachel looked at Nathan.

— Are you sure it's here?

Nathan nodded.

" Alvarez never stays in one place very long. But if anyone knows anything about Royce, it's him."

Hayes looked at the house in the distance.

— It doesn't look like a hospitable place.

Eleanor drew her gun and checked the magazine.

— Nowhere is hospitable to us.

Nathan parked in front of the house and got out of the car.

— Stay alert. Alvarez trusts only one person – himself.

*****

The door of the house opened before they had a chance to knock.

On the porch stood Miguel Alvarez , a medium-height man with a stern face and a scar running from his temple to his jaw.

He smiled slightly.

—Bishop .

Nathan looked at him.

—Miguel .

Alvarez leaned against the doorframe.

— I didn't think I'd ever see you again.

Rachel looked at Nathan.

— Do you still trust this man?

Alvarez looked at her with amusement.

— That's a good question.

Nathan sighed.

— We don't have time for games, Miguel. We're looking for Royce.

Alvarez looked at them for a moment, then nodded.

— Come in. But leave your weapons at the door.

Rachel looked at Nathan.

— I don't like it from the very beginning.

Nathan smiled slightly.

— That means we're in the right place.

Inside, the house was modest but well secured.

Alvarez poured himself a shot of tequila and looked at Nathan.

— So you're looking for Royce.

Nathan nodded.

— Do you know where he is?

Alvarez smiled slightly.

— Of course. But that's not a question you should be asking me.

Rachel looked at him.

— So what question should we ask you?

Alvarez looked her straight in the eye.

— Why is Royce here?

Eleanor frowned.

— We thought he was running away.

Alvarez laughed quietly.

— He ran away?

He took a sip of tequila.

— No. He's building something here.

Nathan stared at Alvarez.

- What do you mean?

Alvarez put down his glass and leaned forward.

" Royce didn't run to Mexico to hide. He came here to start something new."

Rachel looked at Nathan.

— What exactly?

Alvarez reached into the drawer and pulled out the photos.

One of them showed a modern complex in the middle of the jungle.

Hayes looked at the photo.

- What is this?

Alvarez looked at him.

— New system base.

Nathan looked at the photos carefully.

— It looks like a private city.

Alvarez nodded.

— Because that's how it is.

Rachel narrowed her eyes.

— He's building his own fortress.

Nathan looked at her.

— And if we let him, no one will stop him.

Eleanor looked at Alvarez.

— Where is it?

Alvarez sighed and pointed to the map.

— Deep in the jungle. No one goes there unless they're invited.

Hayes looked at Rachel and Nathan.

— And of course we intend to go in there.

Nathan nodded.

- Of course.

Alvarez leaned on the table.

— You know this is a suicide mission, right?

Rachel looked at Nathan.

— We've had nothing to lose for a long time.

Nathan smiled slightly.

— So it's time to end this once and for all.

*****

Four hours later they were driving towards the jungle.

Rachel looked at Nathan.

— What are our options?

Nathan looked at the map.

— One.

Hayes looked at him.

— Go in there and get him.

Eleanor looked out the window.

— It won't be easy.

Nathan looked at her.

— It wasn't supposed to be.

The jungle was quiet. Too quiet.

Nathan looked at Rachel.

— Something is wrong.

Hayes checked the GPS.

— We are close.

Eleanor looked at Nathan.

" If Royce knows we're here..."

Nathan clenched his jaw.

— That means he's already waiting for us.

They entered the valley and saw Royce's compound.

Rachel looked at Nathan.

— This is bigger than I thought.

Nathan pulled out his gun.

— So let's make sure it doesn't survive.

*****

Nathan, Rachel, Eleanor, and Hayes lay on a hill overlooking the Royce compound.

It was huge. Enclosed by a high wall, with watchtowers at each corner. It resembled a private fortress.

Rachel looked through the binoculars.

— This is no ordinary shelter. This is a base of operations.

Hayes checked the satellite maps.

— The structure looks modern. Surveillance, gun turrets, even a signal jamming system.

Eleanor narrowed her eyes.

— So Royce had everything planned here long ago.

Nathan looked at the complex.

— That means if we don't do anything now, we'll never have a second chance.

Rachel looked at him.

— How do we get there?

Nathan pointed to a small side building.

" This looks like a supply point. If they get supplies today, we can hook up with transport."

Hayes looked at the map.

— The next delivery is scheduled for tomorrow morning.

Eleanor put down her binoculars.

— So we have a dozen or so hours to figure out how to get there without getting killed.

Nathan looked at Rachel.

— We have to act quickly.

Rachel smiled slightly.

— So it's time for the jump of a lifetime.

They sat in a makeshift hideout a few kilometers from the complex, analyzing the plan.

Hayes pointed out a side entrance on the map.

" They're delivering food and supplies here. We can take over one of the shipments."

Eleanor looked at Nathan.

— What if Royce knows someone is hunting him?

Nathan sighed.

— He knows that for sure. But he doesn't know that we are so close.

Rachel looked at Hayes.

— Do you have a way to disrupt the monitoring?

Hayes smiled.

— Sure. But it will only work for a few minutes.

Nathan looked at everyone.

— That's all we need.

The next morning they were waiting on the road leading to the complex.

The delivery truck arrived on time.

Rachel looked at Nathan.

- Ready?

Nathan nodded.

— Let's do it.

As the vehicle slowed before the checkpoint, Nathan and Rachel jumped out of hiding and jumped into the back of the truck.

Eleanor and Hayes waited in the distance, ready to intercept the surveillance signal.

The truck drove through the gate.

Rachel looked at Nathan.

— It's now or never.

Military order prevailed inside the complex.

Nathan and Rachel got out of the truck and hid behind the crates.

Hayes spoke into the receiver.

— You have five minutes before the cameras come back.

Rachel looked at Nathan.

— Where to now?

Nathan looked at the main building.

" If Royce's here, he'll be inside."

Eleanor spoke on the radio.

— But it won't be easy.

Nathan smiled slightly.

— It never is.

They moved carefully through the complex.

Rachel glanced at the guards patrolling the courtyard.

— Too many people.

Nathan glanced at the service door on the left.

— Over there. We can get in undetected.

Hayes spoke into the receiver.

— Quick. Cameras will be back in two minutes.

Rachel and Nathan ran to the door and slipped inside.

It was dark and quiet inside.

Nathan looked at Rachel.

— Now let's find Royce.

They moved carefully through narrow corridors.

Rachel looked at Nathan.

— We need to get to the administration office. We'll find answers there.

Nathan looked at the door marked **"MAIN CONTROL. "**

— This should help us.

Rachel opened the door.

They went inside and saw servers and surveillance screens.

Nathan looked at the computers.

— Hayes, are you with us?

Hayes answered the phone.

— Connect me to the system.

Rachel plugged Hayes' device into the computer.

After a moment, files appeared on the screen.

— I have it.

Nathan looked at the screen.

— Where's Royce?

Hayes scrolled through the data.

— Third floor, private apartment.

Rachel looked at Nathan.

— That's where we're going.

Nathan and Rachel left the monitoring center and headed for the stairs.

When they were on the second floor, they heard footsteps.

Rachel tugged on Nathan's arm.

— Someone is coming.

They hid behind a pillar.

The elevator doors opened and William Royce stepped into the hallway.

Nathan held his breath.

Royce was here.

Rachel looked at Nathan.

— This is our chance.

Nathan looked at Royce.

— We're going for him.

Royce walked down the hall, talking on the phone.

Nathan and Rachel followed him, keeping to the shadows.

As Royce opened the door to his apartment, Nathan sped up.

He lunged at him, knocking him to the floor.

Royce fell with a bang.

— What the hell...?!

Rachel aimed the gun at his head.

— It's over, Royce.

Royce looked at them and... smiled.

— No, my dears. This is just the beginning.

Nathan grabbed Royce by the shirt and lifted him up.

— You have nowhere to run anymore.

Royce looked him in the eye.

— Do you think I'm the problem?

Rachel frowned.

- What do you mean?

Royce smiled slightly.

— There is someone greater. Someone who has always stood in the shadows.

Nathan looked at Rachel.

— Who are you talking about?

Royce leaned toward them and whispered one word:

— Wren.

*****

Nathan looked at Royce with icy calm.

— Wren?

Royce smiled slightly, though his eyes showed weariness.

— You always thought I was the main player. But I was just the manager...

Rachel narrowed her eyes.

—And Wren was the owner.

Royce nodded.

" He built all this. He controls the government, the military, the finances. You think my money came from politics? No. Wren paid me to do what I did."

Nathan squeezed his shirt.

— Where is he?

Royce laughed quietly.

— You'll never find him.

Rachel pulled out her gun and pulled back the bolt.

— Do you want to find out?

Royce looked at her and sighed.

" Wren is untouchable. Even if you find him, he's already anticipated it."

Nathan narrowed his eyes.

— What did he predict?

Royce looked him in the eye.

— That I will kill you here.

At that moment the apartment door exploded.

The shock wave threw Nathan and Rachel to the floor.

Four armed men in black uniforms rushed inside .

Royce dropped to the floor and crawled toward the desk.

Nathan pulled out his gun, but one of the attackers kicked him in the hand, knocking the gun away.

Rachel stood up and lunged at one of them, kneeing him in the stomach.

But it was an ambush.

Before they could react, they were overpowered.

Nathan felt a plastic band tighten around his neck.

He heard Royce's voice.

— I told you. This is just the beginning.

And then everything went dark.

*****

Nathan woke up tied to a chair.

There was silence in the room, interrupted only by the monotonous sound of the fans.

Rachel sat across from him, also feeling self-conscious.

"Where are we? " she asked, looking around the dark room.

Nathan looked at the one-way mirror.

— Probably in some underground complex.

The door opened and Alexander Wren walked in .

Dressed in an elegant suit, calm, composed.

He looked at Nathan with curiosity.

— Well, Mr. Bishop. You've come a long way to get here.

Rachel looked at him coldly.

— You are behind all this.

Wren smiled slightly.

— Yes. And I'll tell you something else.

He stepped closer.

— You never had a chance.

Nathan looked at Wren with icy determination.

— That's interesting, because we're still here.

Wren spread his hands.

— Yes. And that's what intrigues me.

Rachel narrowed her eyes.

— Why didn't you kill us?

Wren smiled slightly.

— Because you can still be useful to me.

Nathan looked at Rachel.

— What are you talking about?

Wren stepped closer to them.

— The system always needs new leaders.

Rachel laughed coldly.

— Do you want to recruit us?

Wren looked at her calmly.

— No. I want to give you a choice.

Nathan narrowed his eyes.

- What?

Wren turned and looked at them over his shoulder.

— Either you join me. Or you disappear.

Nathan looked at Rachel.

Rachel looked at Wren.

— We're disappearing? Does that mean you'll kill us?

Wren smiled slightly.

— I don't have to. If you refuse, you'll disappear in the worst possible way. The world will forget you ever existed.

Nathan narrowed his eyes.

— And you think we will choose the first option?

Wren sighed.

— I hoped you were smarter than that.

Rachel looked at Nathan.

— I don't choose any of these options.

Wren looked at her.

— Then... you will have to suffer the consequences.

He nodded and the door opened.

Two guards entered.

Nathan looked at Rachel.

— Do you have a plan?

Rachel smiled slightly.

- Of course.

And then she kicked the guard right in the knee.

The confusion lasted only a few seconds.

Rachel knocked over one guard, and Nathan head-butted the other one against the wall.

Wren backed toward the door.

— It was a mistake.

Nathan tore off the plastic handcuffs and grabbed the guard's gun.

He aimed straight at Wren.

— Not so fast.

Wren looked at him calmly.

— If you kill me, the arrangement will still survive.

Rachel picked up the other guard's weapon.

— But you don't anymore.

Wren smiled slightly.

- We'll see.

And then the light in the room went out.

Nathan and Rachel rushed forward, but Wren was already gone.

The door was open.

Rachel looked at Nathan.

— He escaped.

Nathan gritted his teeth.

— Not for long.

Hayes spoke into the receiver.

— What's going on?! We've lost you!

Nathan looked at Rachel.

" Wren is the real boss of the system. We have to get to him."

Eleanor spoke over the radio.

— We have a problem.

Nathan looked at her.

- What's going on?

Eleanor took a deep breath.

— The entire complex is on its feet. If you don't get out now, you won't get out at all.

Rachel looked at Nathan.

— What are we doing?

Nathan loaded the gun.

— Let's finish this.

*****

Nathan and Rachel ran from the room, weapons ready.

The entire Royce complex was on its feet.

Sirens wailed and guards moved through the corridors, looking for intruders.

Hayes spoke into the receiver.

— You have exactly three minutes before all exits are closed.

Rachel looked at Nathan.

" We can't just run away. We have to find Wren."

Nathan looked at the stairs leading to the upper floor.

— If he hasn't escaped yet, he'll be on the roof.

Eleanor spoke over the radio.

— The helicopter is landing there now.

Rachel looked at Nathan.

— So that's where we must be.

They ran up the stairs, taking two steps at a time.

Rachel glanced at her watch.

— Two minutes.

Hayes shouted into the radio.

" Hurry up! If they close the roof, you can't get to Wren!"

Nathan opened the door to the top floor and saw a group of guards blocking the entrance to the roof.

Rachel looked at him.

— We don't have time for subtlety.

Nathan nodded.

- I agree.

He pulled out his gun and shot at an electrical box on the wall.

The lights went out.

The guards started screaming.

Rachel lunged at the nearest one, kneeing him in the ribs.

Nathan overpowered the other and kicked open the door to the roof.

They ran straight towards the helicopter.

*****

Alexander Wren stood on the roof, wearing a long coat, talking on a satellite phone.

Next to him are two security guards armed with assault rifles.

As Nathan and Rachel crashed onto the roof, Wren looked at them and smiled slightly.

— Impressive.

Rachel raised her gun.

— It's over, Wren.

Wren sighed and glanced at his watch.

- I don't think so.

Nathan looked at the helicopter. The pilot was already in the cockpit, the engines starting to rev.

— We won't let you escape.

Wren looked at them with cold calm.

— Why do you still think I'm running away?

Rachel frowned.

- What do you mean?

Wren smiled slightly.

— You think you came for me. And I was waiting for you.

Nathan felt a cold shiver run down his spine.

And then the door behind them slammed shut with a bang.

Nathan and Rachel whirled around.

Four more guards ran onto the roof, blocking their escape route.

Wren slowly walked toward them.

— Did you think you could stop me?

Nathan looked him straight in the eye.

— We are going to do it.

Wren smiled slightly.

— No, Mr. Bishop. I just won.

Rachel looked at him.

— Why? Because you have several guards?

Wren shook his head.

— No. Because right now, at this very moment, in Washington, the FBI has officially designated you as terrorists.

Nathan frowned.

- What?

Wren pulled out his phone and showed them a live feed from CNN.

The presenter spoke in a calm tone:

"Nathan Bishop, Rachel Price and Eleanor Price are wanted in connection with the attempted assassination of senior government officials."

Rachel looked at the screen, feeling herself go cold.

— It's impossible…

Nathan clenched his fists.

— You knew we would come here.

Wren nodded.

— Of course. And that's why your fight is over.

Nathan looked at Rachel.

— No. It's not over yet.

Wren looked at him with amusement.

— Really? What's your plan now?

Nathan glanced at Rachel.

— Improvisation.

And then he lunged at Wren.

Nathan punched Wren in the face, sending him to the ground.

Rachel drew her gun and fired at the guards, forcing them to take cover.

Wren shouted:

— Shoot them!

Nathan looked at the helicopter.

Rachel screamed:

—Bishop, no!

But Nathan was already running.

He grabbed the helicopter's landing gear and pulled himself inside.

The pilot looked at him in horror.

Nathan pulled out his gun and shot him square in the leg.

The helicopter began to wobble.

Rachel rushed for cover, trying to avoid the bullets.

Wren stood up, holding his bleeding lip.

— Shoot him down!

The guards raised their weapons.

Rachel looked at the helicopter as it began to rise.

—Nathan!

Nathan looked at her.

— Finish this!

And then the helicopter took off, taking him with it.

*****

Rachel watched the helicopter fly away.

Eleanor spoke into the receiver.

- What's going on?!

Rachel clenched her jaw.

— Nathan flew away in a helicopter.

Hayes shouted into the radio.

- What?!

Rachel looked at Wren, who was holding his split lip and smiling slightly.

— Well, it looks like your friend just made a big mistake.

Rachel raised the gun and aimed it at his head.

- Shut up.

Eleanor screamed into the radio.

— Rachel, we have to get out of there!

Rachel took a deep breath and looked at Wren.

— It's not over yet.

She turned and headed toward the edge of the roof, where an escape rope awaited her.

The guards opened fire.

But Rachel was already jumping.

Nathan was hanging on the helicopter's landing gear, holding on to the metal beam with all his might.

The wind whipped across his face and engines roared overhead.

Inside the cockpit, the pilot groaned in pain, holding his shot leg.

Nathan pulled himself up and slid inside the machine.

— Land. Now.

The pilot looked at him in horror.

— I can't! I have orders to fly to...

Nathan put the barrel to his temple.

- Now.

The pilot swallowed and grabbed the controls.

The helicopter slowly began to lose altitude.

But then Nathan heard movement behind him.

He turned just in time to see a guard emerge from the rear compartment, knife in hand.

Nathan threw himself to the side, avoiding the first blow.

The guard was fast and well trained.

Nathan delivered a blow to the ribs, but the man merely stepped back and swung the knife again.

The helicopter rocked.

Nathan took a step back and hit the control panel with his elbow.

The lights in the cabin flickered.

The pilot shouted:

— What the hell are you doing?!

The guard tried again, but Nathan grabbed his wrist and twisted it back.

The knife fell to the floor.

Nathan head-butted him and pushed him against the door.

But the guard still didn't give up.

He began to reach for the gun at his belt.

Nathan kicked him square in the chest, sending him flying into the open door of the helicopter.

The man flew down.

Nathan looked after him, watching him disappear into the jungle below.

He turned to the pilot.

— Now land if you don't want to end up like him.

*****

Rachel jumped from the roof onto the rope and dropped to the lower level of the complex.

Behind her she heard the guards shouting.

— Stop her!

But she was already running.

Eleanor spoke over the radio:

— Rachel, you have three options. Two are already closed.

Rachel looked at the map.

— And the third?

Hayes interjected:

— It's an underground tunnel leading to the landing site.

Rachel rushed towards it, jumping over the bodies of the guards she had previously overpowered.

As she reached the tunnel entrance, the doors began to close.

She accelerated.

She threw herself at the last moment, slipping under the falling gate.

It worked.

She got up and continued running.

She had to find Nathan.

The helicopter landed in a small clearing in the jungle.

Nathan opened the door and pulled the pilot by the collar.

— Get out.

The pilot fell to his knees, still holding his leg.

Nathan looked at the horizon.

He had to go back to Rachel.

But before he could move, he heard a familiar voice.

— Not so fast, Bishop.

He turned around slowly.

William Royce stood before him, surrounded by six armed men.

Royce smiled slightly.

— It's nice to see you.

Nathan clenched his fists.

—Royce.

The man spread his arms.

— Did you think it was over?

Nathan looked at his men.

— If you want to kill me, just do it.

Royce shook his head.

—No, Nathan. I don't want to kill you.

He took a step closer.

— I want to recruit you.

*****

Rachel ran through the tunnel, gun at the ready.

Eleanor shouted over the radio:

— Rachel, the guards are already looking for you!

Rachel picked up her pace.

— Where is Nathan?!

Hayes replied:

— His helicopter landed about two miles to the south.

Rachel ran out of the tunnel and looked at the road leading into the jungle.

— Find me transportation.

Eleanor hesitated.

— It's dangerous.

Rachel loaded the magazine.

— I don't care. I have to find him.

Nathan looked at Royce.

— I will never join you.

Royce smiled slightly.

" Really? What if I told you Wren has already lost?"

Nathan narrowed his eyes.

- What do you mean?

Royce stepped closer.

—Wren thought he had control of the system. But he made one mistake.

Nathan looked him in the eye.

- What?

Royce smiled wider.

— He allowed me to survive.

Nathan began to understand.

— You're the one who wants to take over the deal.

Royce nodded.

— And I want you to be a part of it.

Nathan laughed coldly.

- Never.

Royce shook his head.

— I thought you would say that.

He nodded to his men.

— So I'll give you one more chance.

Nathan looked at his guards.

- What?

Royce smiled.

" Either you join me or Rachel dies."

*****

Nathan stared at Royce, feeling his fists slowly clench.

— If you touch her, I'll kill you.

Royce smiled slightly, as if he knew exactly what he was about to hear.

—Oh, Nathan. You're so predictable.

One of his guards walked over and handed him a tablet. Royce lifted the screen so Nathan could see.

Rachel was on the screen.

Tied up. Held by two armed men.

Her face was bloody, but her eyes were full of anger.

Nathan felt a cold, icy rage clench in his stomach.

Rachel spoke first:

— Don't listen to him, Nathan!

Royce turned the tablet towards himself and sighed.

— Well, he's got nerve. But that's nothing new.

He looked at Nathan.

— So? What will you decide?

Rachel tried to break free, but the man holding her arms tightened his grip.

— Let me out, you son of a bitch.

One of the guards punched her in the stomach.

Rachel cringed, coughing, but she didn't give them the satisfaction of showing her pain.

Wren stood in the corner of the room, observing everything with cool detachment.

"I wonder, Miss Price, how much Bishop is willing to sacrifice to save you."

Rachel looked at him with contempt.

— You don't know Nathan.

Wren smiled slightly.

— I know him better than you think.

He turned to the guards.

— If she doesn't decide within an hour, kill her.

Nathan looked at Royce, trying to contain his anger.

— What do you want me to do?

Royce adjusted his jacket cuffs.

— The system needs a new leader.

Nathan snorted.

— I thought you were taking over.

Royce smiled.

— I'm just a player. You can be the face.

Nathan shook his head.

- Never.

Royce sighed.

— I thought you would say that.

He waved at the guard.

" Call them. If Bishop won't cooperate, Rachel won't live long."

Nathan closed his eyes for a second.

He had to do something.

*****

Eleanor and Hayes were in a hidden van several miles from the complex.

Eleanor glanced at her laptop screen where she could still see Nathan's GPS signal.

— Something is wrong.

Hayes looked at her.

- What do you mean?

Eleanor took a deep breath.

" Royce shouldn't have let Nathan live. He's up to something."

Hayes nodded.

—And that means Rachel is in danger too.

Eleanor looked at the map.

" We have to get to them before Royce causes a tragedy."

Hayes smiled slightly.

— So we'll do it the old-fashioned way?

Eleanor nodded.

— Yes. We'll break in.

*****

Rachel felt blood trickle down her lip, but she ignored the pain.

The guards looked at her without emotion.

One of them spoke:

— Last chance.

Rachel spat on the floor.

— Fuck you.

The guard raised his weapon.

And then there was an explosion.

The wall shook and dust and debris filled the room.

The door opened with a bang.

Rachel glanced at the entrance.

Eleanor and Hayes stood in the doorway, armed, ready to fight.

Eleanor smiled.

— Hey, honey. Do you need a ride?

*****

Royce looked at his phone when he received the message.

The guard leaned over to him and whispered:

— Rachel ran away.

Nathan saw Royce's face change for a moment.

He lost control.

Nathan took advantage of this moment and lunged at the guard next to him.

He grabbed him by the wrist and turned the gun towards him.

A shot was fired.

The second guard fell dead.

Nathan punched the first one in the face, grabbed the gun from him and aimed it at Royce.

— Game over.

Royce moved away slowly.

—Bishop ... don't do this.

Nathan looked at him with cold calm.

— For twenty years the system has manipulated this country. And now it is ending.

Royce stepped back even further.

— If you kill me, you'll never know who's really at the top.

Nathan didn't move.

— I don't care.

And then Royce lunged sideways and pressed a hidden button on the wall.

The entire building shook.

The alarms sounded again.

Royce looked at Nathan and smiled.

— I always have a backup plan.

Nathan looked up and saw the metal door beginning to fall.

The whole place was about to close down.

Rachel ran down the hall, Eleanor and Hayes close behind her.

— Where's Nathan?!

Hayes glanced at his watch.

— Its GPS signal is inside!

Rachel stopped and looked at the metal doors lowering into the main hallway.

— If it closes, it won't come out!

Eleanor looked at Rachel.

— So, what do we do?

Rachel looked at them, then at the door.

And she started running.

*****

Rachel ran at breakneck speed, ignoring the screams of Eleanor and Hayes behind her.

The metal door fell lower and lower.

If he doesn't make it, Nathan will be imprisoned.

She gritted her teeth and threw herself to the ground, sliding under the heavy steel plate at the last second.

The door slammed behind her with a deafening bang.

Inside the complex, the air smelled of burning and dust.

Rachel looked around, keeping her gun raised.

—Nathan?!

She heard footsteps in the distance.

And then she saw him.

He stood a few meters away, gun in hand, and in front of him was William Royce, kneeling on the floor, with his hands tied.

Rachel looked at Nathan.

His face was tense, his eyes as cold as steel.

— You've got it.

Nathan didn't take his eyes off Royce.

— Yes. And now we're deciding what to do with him.

Royce looked at them with a slight smile, even though his lip was bloody.

— Do you really think you'll kill me?

Rachel raised her gun.

— We don't think. We know.

Royce sighed as if the whole situation was amusing to him.

— If you kill me, it won't change anything.

Nathan narrowed his eyes.

— It will change everything.

Royce laughed quietly.

— No. Because the deal doesn't end with me.

Rachel looked at Nathan.

— We shouldn't listen to him.

Nathan was silent for a moment.

Then he walked up to Royce and put the barrel of the gun to his temple.

Royce smiled.

— Do it. But before you do it, I want to tell you one thing.

Nathan didn't look down.

— You have ten seconds.

Royce leaned forward slightly.

— Wren is not at the top.

Rachel stiffened.

— You're lying.

Royce looked at her.

— No. Wren's just another player. Just like me. But there's someone above him.

Nathan narrowed his eyes.

- Who?

Royce smiled.

— If you kill me, you'll never know.

Rachel looked at Nathan.

— We can't trust him.

Nathan didn't speak for a moment.

Then he looked at Royce and hit him in the face with the butt of the gun.

Royce fell to the floor, bleeding from the nose.

— You're staying alive. For now.

Rachel looked at Nathan.

- Why?

Nathan holstered his gun.

— Because if he's telling the truth, we just found the real leader of the system.

*****

Eleanor and Hayes waited on the other side of the door, listening for the sounds of gunfire.

Eleanor looked at Hayes.

— If we don't open that door, it could stay there forever.

Hayes typed something into his laptop.

— Give me a minute.

Eleanor drew her gun.

— We don't have a minute.

Hayes looked at her and sighed.

— Okay. The old way.

He connected the device to the door controller and pressed enter.

The doors began to open.

Eleanor raised her gun and stepped inside.

She found Rachel and Nathan above Royce.

— I guess we missed the fun.

Rachel smiled slightly.

- Not yet.

Nathan looked at Eleanor.

— We have to get to Wren.

Eleanor frowned.

—I thought Royce was the target.

Nathan looked at Royce.

— He's just a dead end.

Rachel looked at Eleanor.

— The system has one more head.

Eleanor raised an eyebrow.

— So now we're hunting someone bigger?

Nathan nodded.

— Yes.

Hayes looked at everyone.

— So who the hell is at the top?

Nathan looked at Royce.

— Speak.

Royce looked at him, bleeding from the mouth.

- I can't.

Rachel aimed the gun at him.

— It wasn't a request.

Royce laughed lightly.

— You don't understand. This is not one man.

Nathan narrowed his eyes.

- What does it mean?

Royce looked him straight in the eye.

— It's an entire organization. A group that controls everything.

Eleanor looked at Hayes.

— He's talking about something bigger than an arrangement.

Hayes started searching on his laptop.

— It's impossible.

Rachel looked at Royce.

— What's his name?

Royce looked at her.

And then he whispered one word:

—**Concordia.**

Rachel frowned.

— What is Concordia?

Royce smiled slightly.

— That which you will never destroy.

Nathan looked at Eleanor.

— Have you heard about it?

Eleanor shook her head.

— No. But if Royce is telling the truth, that means the deal was just part of something bigger.

Hayes looked at the screen.

— There's nothing about Concordia online. No connections, no documents. It's like a ghost.

Nathan looked at Royce.

— Who governs them?

Royce smiled.

— You're asking the wrong questions.

Rachel narrowed her eyes.

— So what questions should we ask?

Royce looked at her.

— Not who governs them.

He paused.

— Only how far their power reaches.

*****

Nathan looked at Royce, trying to tell if he was lying.

—Concordia.

He repeated the word slowly, as if weighing it in his mind.

Rachel narrowed her eyes.

— I've never heard of that.

Royce smiled slightly, even though his lip was split and blood was still dripping from it.

— And that's why you'll never find them.

Nathan grabbed him by the collar and pulled him closer.

— Who governs them?

Royce sighed as if he was talking to a child.

— You're asking the wrong questions.

Nathan pressed the barrel of the gun to his forehead.

— So what questions should I ask?

Royce looked him straight in the eye.

— Who works for them.

Eleanor looked at Hayes, who was searching databases on his laptop.

— Nothing. Zero. There's no mention of Concordia.

Hayes shook his head.

— It's impossible. Every organization leaves a trace.

Royce laughed quietly.

— Concordia has been around for decades. They are invisible because they want to be.

Rachel looked at Nathan.

— If this is true, we are in even greater danger than we thought.

Nathan took a deep breath.

— So how do we find them?

Royce looked at him with a hint of a smile.

— They will find you first.

*****

At that moment, something flashed on Hayes' screen.

— Wait... I have something.

Rachel stepped closer.

- What is this?

Hayes swiped his finger across the screen.

—Old CIA documents. Classification: Top Secret.

Nathan looked at the monitor.

- Year?

Hayes frowned.

— 1954.

Rachel looked at Nathan.

— Concordia has existed for over seventy years?

Hayes nodded.

—And it looks like they started at the CIA.

Royce looked at the screen and smiled slightly.

— Well, look. Maybe you're not as stupid as I thought.

Rachel looked at him sharply.

" So this is intelligence? The CIA controls Concordia?"

Royce shook his head.

— No. Concordia is controlled by the CIA.

Nathan looked at Royce in disbelief.

— Are you telling me that the entire American intelligence agency is just a puppet?

Royce nodded.

— Yes. And not just the CIA. The Pentagon, Wall Street, Congress. They're the ones pulling the strings.

Rachel looked at Nathan.

— This is no longer just an arrangement. It is a government in the shadows.

Nathan felt a knot in his stomach.

— So who's at the top?

Royce smiled slightly.

— Do you really want to know?

Eleanor raised her gun.

— Speak.

Royce sighed.

—Sir Jonathan Calloway.

There was silence.

Rachel looked at Eleanor.

— Calloway? Former presidential adviser?

Nathan frowned.

— We thought he was dead.

Royce shook his head.

— Only officially.

Nathan looked at Hayes.

— Find me everything you can on Calloway.

Hayes entered the name into the databases.

After a moment he looked up.

— There is nothing.

Rachel frowned.

— What? He was an advisor to the president. There has to be some trace.

Hayes shook his head.

— No. There is nothing. No documents, no records. As if he never existed.

Eleanor looked at Royce.

— What is he doing now?

Royce smiled.

— He rules the world.

Nathan turned to Rachel.

" If Royce is telling the truth, Calloway is alive and atop Concordia."

Rachel nodded.

— So if we find him…

Eleanor finished for her.

— We can destroy everything.

Royce laughed quietly.

— Do you really think it's that simple?

Nathan looked at him coldly.

" If Calloway's alive, we'll find him."

Royce shook his head.

— No. Because he'll find you first.

At that moment an alarm sounded over Hayes's earpiece.

— Something is happening.

Nathan looked at him.

- What?

Hayes looked at the screen.

— Someone spotted us.

Rachel looked at Royce.

— Is that you?

Royce smiled.

— No. It's Calloway.

Nathan looked at Eleanor.

— We have to get out of here. Now.

Hayes quickly began packing his gear.

Rachel looked at Royce.

— Are we taking him?

Nathan looked at him for a moment.

- NO.

Rachel narrowed her eyes.

— We leave him here?

Nathan stood up and looked at Royce.

"Calloway will find him anyway."

Royce smiled slightly.

—You just made a mistake, Bishop.

Nathan looked at Rachel.

— Let's go.

They left the room, leaving Royce alone.

And Royce watched them go, smiling to himself.

— Now the real game begins…

*****

Nathan, Rachel, Eleanor, and Hayes ran through the halls of the complex, past dead guards and still flashing red alarm lights.

Hayes looked at the phone.

— We have five minutes before they get here.

Nathan kept running.

- Who?

Hayes looked at him worriedly.

— I don't know, but the lock signal is coming from Langley.

Rachel looked at Eleanor.

—CIA?

Eleanor nodded.

" It can't be a coincidence. If Calloway's alive, he's the one who sent men after us."

Nathan turned into a side corridor.

— We have to get out of here. Now.

They ran to the hidden elevator that Eleanor had found earlier in the building's plans.

Hayes glanced at the control panel.

— This leads to the escape tunnel.

Rachel looked at Nathan.

" If Calloway's spotted us, they're probably already waiting outside."

Nathan pressed the button.

— So we have to be faster.

The elevator doors opened and everyone ran inside.

Hayes closed the control panel.

— We go down 40 meters underground.

Eleanor looked at Nathan.

— And then what?

Nathan looked at her coldly.

— We'll find Calloway and we'll end this.

The elevator stopped at the bottom level and the doors opened onto a long, narrow tunnel leading to the exit.

Rachel looked at Hayes.

— Does this lead outside?

Hayes nodded.

— Yes. 500 meters straight.

Nathan emerged first, holding his weapon at the ready.

— We are not stopping.

They ran through the darkness, their footsteps echoing off the concrete walls.

After a few minutes they saw light at the end of the tunnel.

Rachel looked at Nathan.

— Almost there.

And then the light went out.

There was silence.

Eleanor drew her gun.

— It's a trap.

Nathan looked at Rachel.

— Someone locked us in here.

Hayes quickly began tinkering with his laptop.

— The GPS signal is gone. Someone has cut off our access to the network.

Nathan clenched his fists.

"Calloway knew we'd be running away this way."

Rachel looked at Eleanor.

— What now?

Eleanor looked around.

— If we stop here, we'll end up like Royce.

Hayes suddenly raised his head.

— Do you hear that?

Rachel held her breath.

In the distance came the sound of heavy boots hitting concrete.

Someone was following them.

And they were not alone.

Nathan raised his gun.

— How many are there?

Hayes looked into the darkness.

— Judging by the steps? At least ten.

Rachel took a deep breath.

— We don't have enough ammo for ten.

Nathan looked at her.

— So we shoot accurately.

Eleanor pulled the zipper back.

- Always.

And then the shooting started.

The bullets struck the concrete walls, shattering bricks and sending clouds of dust into the air.

Rachel threw herself behind a metal crate and fired three shots at the attackers.

Two fell.

Nathan raised his gun and hit the third one.

But they kept coming.

Hayes shouted:

— We have a problem!

Eleanor looked at him.

— What is it?

Hayes pointed to the exit.

— Someone is closing the gate!

Nathan glanced at the end of the tunnel.

The metal grate slowly fell, blocking the only escape route.

Rachel looked at Eleanor.

— If we don't make it in time...

Nathan was already running.

— There is no "if."

Nathan lunged forward, ignoring the arrows whistling above his head.

The gate fell faster and faster.

Rachel and Eleanor ran close behind him.

Hayes tried to type something into the computer, but the system did not respond.

— I can't stop it!

Nathan saw the last gap under the gate.

He didn't hesitate.

He lunged forward and slid through to the other side just before it closed.

Rachel grabbed the edge at the last second.

Eleanor and Hayes are stuck on the other side.

Rachel tried to pull Eleanor up, but it was too late.

The gate slammed shut with a loud bang.

Eleanor looked through the metal bars.

— Go!

Rachel shook her head.

— We won't leave you!

Nathan looked at her.

— We have no choice.

Another wave of guards approached from behind.

Eleanor looked at Rachel and smiled slightly.

— Find Calloway.

Hayes added:

— And finish it.

And then the shooting started again.

Rachel held her breath as she watched Eleanor and Hayes disappear into cover, trying to defend themselves.

Nathan grabbed her hand.

— We have to go. Now.

Rachel clenched her fists, then looked at him.

— We'll finish this.

Nathan nodded.

— We'll finish it.

They turned and began to run towards the darkness.

A few miles away, in a luxurious residence in Geneva, Sir Jonathan Calloway stood on a balcony, looking out over the illuminated city.

Behind him stood a tall man in an elegant suit.

—Bishop and Price survived.

Calloway sighed and looked at his glass of wine.

— Of course they survived.

He looked at his advisor.

— But that doesn't matter.

The man frowned.

- Why?

Calloway smiled slightly.

— Because they still don't understand that they never had a chance to win.

*****

Nathan and Rachel ran through the jungle, their footsteps muffled by the damp earth.

shots were still heard.

Rachel glanced over her shoulder, her thoughts drifting to Eleanor and Hayes.

— We have to go back for them.

Nathan grabbed her hand and pulled her sideways, toward a hidden path.

— We can't.

Rachel looked at him angrily.

—Nathan …

Nathan stopped and looked her straight in the eyes.

" They knew what they were doing. If we stay, we'll all die."

Rachel gritted her teeth, but after a moment she nodded.

—So let's find Calloway and end this.

Nathan nodded.

" Hayes left us a trail. Now we have to follow it."

They turned around and began to run towards the designated evacuation point.

They had no idea that Calloway was already waiting for them.

*****

Geneva, Switzerland.

Sir Jonathan Calloway sat in his luxurious apartment, twirling a glass of whiskey in his fingers.

Opposite him stood Alexander Wren.

Wren looked at him worriedly.

" Royce's been captured. Eleanor and Hayes are trapped. But Bishop and Price survived."

Calloway smiled slightly.

— Of course they survived.

Wren tensed.

— You're not worried?

Calloway looked up.

— Why should I be?

Wren narrowed his eyes.

— They are closer to the truth than anyone before.

Calloway put down his glass and leaned back in his chair.

— And that's why we'll do what we always do.

Wren looked at him questioningly.

Calloway smiled slightly.

" We don't have to kill them. We have to make sure no one believes them."

Nathan and Rachel reached a hidden cabin in the mountains where they would meet Hayes' contact.

Nathan entered first, holding his gun at the ready.

— There's no one here.

Rachel closed the door behind her.

— Are we waiting?

Nathan looked at his watch.

— We'll give them an hour.

Rachel sat down at the table, trying to calm her breathing.

— What if it's a trap?

Nathan looked at her.

— Then we fight.

Suddenly someone knocked on the door.

Nathan and Rachel looked at each other.

Rachel drew her gun.

Nathan walked to the door and opened it slowly.

In front of him stood Miguel Alvarez.

Nathan narrowed his eyes.

— What are you doing here?

Alvarez smiled slightly.

— You're asking the wrong questions.

He went inside and threw a flash drive on the table.

— This is your only chance to survive.

Rachel looked at him suspiciously.

- What is this?

Alvarez sat down and poured himself a glass of water.

— Concordia data. What Royce didn't tell you.

Nathan looked at the flash drive.

— Where did you get that?

Alvarez smiled slightly.

— Let's just say I have old debts to pay off.

Rachel took a deep breath.

— What's on it?

Alvarez looked at her seriously.

— List.

Nathan narrowed his eyes.

— List of what?

Alvarez took a sip of water and looked at them.

— A list of everyone who works for Concordia.

Rachel and Nathan stared at the flash drive on the table.

Rachel swallowed hard.

— List of all?

Alvarez nodded.

— Politicians, military, media people. Judges, corporate CEOs.

Nathan looked at him.

— Calloway?

Alvarez smiled slightly.

— At the very top.

Rachel looked at Nathan.

— If this is true…

Nathan finished for her.

— Then we can overthrow the entire system.

Alvarez sighed.

— Yes. But there is one problem.

Rachel narrowed her eyes.

- What?

Alvarez looked at them seriously.

— If you have this list, it means Concordia already knows you have it.

Nathan looked at Rachel.

— Which means everyone will be after us now.

*****

Geneva, Switzerland.

Calloway sat in his office reading the report from Wren.

Wren stood in front of him, clearly nervous.

—Bishop and Price have a list.

Calloway smiled slightly.

- Excellent.

Wren frowned.

- Excellent?

Calloway looked at him calmly.

— Yes. Because now the whole world will be after them, thinking they're a threat.

Wren swallowed.

— What are we doing?

Calloway put down the report and looked out the window at the Geneva skyline.

" We don't have to do anything. They'll be dead soon."

*****

Nathan stared at the laptop screen where Hayes was decoding files from a flash drive.

Rachel stood nearby, shaking hands.

— Do we have it?

Hayes looked at them in horror.

— This is bigger than I thought.

Nathan looked at the screen.

The list of names went on forever.

Rachel took a deep breath.

— If we make this public…

Nathan looked at her.

— Then we'll break up Concordia forever.

Suddenly the computer started flickering.

Hayes looked at the screen.

— What the hell...?

appeared on the screen.

Nathan and Rachel looked at her in silence.

"Leave it. You have 24 hours. Otherwise, you die."

Rachel looked at Nathan.

— What now?

Nathan looked into her eyes.

— We reveal everything.

And then someone shot through the window.

The glass exploded.

Nathan lunged at Rachel, knocking her to the floor before more bullets slammed into the wall behind them.

Hayes fell over with his laptop, and Eleanor was already drawing her gun.

"Sniper!" she shouted.

Nathan rose to one knee and looked toward the mountainside.

— We have to get out of here!

Rachel reached for her gun and fired several times at the hill, but she knew it was no use.

Hayes was picking up the scattered parts of the laptop.

— We can't leave this!

Nathan grabbed him by the arm.

— It's a matter of life now, Hayes.

More shots tore through the wooden walls of the hut.

Eleanor turned to Nathan.

— Do we have an exit in the back?

Nathan shook his head.

— No. But we have a basement.

Rachel looked at him.

— Basement?

Nathan moved to the small door under the table and opened it.

" It leads to a tunnel under the hill. We have to go. Now!"

Hayes looked at the laptop, then at Nathan, and finally entered first.

Rachel and Eleanor followed him.

Nathan was last.

Before he disappeared, he glanced one more time at the broken window.

They knew where we were.

They ran through a tunnel whose walls were damp with condensation.

Hayes glanced at Nathan.

— How long has this tunnel been here?

Nathan kept running.

— Long. And at the end it has an exit leading to the old road.

Rachel looked at Eleanor.

— And what then?

Eleanor frowned.

— We have to hide.

Hayes shook his head.

— No. We have to get the transmission out.

Nathan stopped and looked at him.

- How?

Hayes lifted the laptop.

" I have a copy of the files. If we can get onto a secure network, we can send it worldwide."

Rachel looked at Nathan.

— But if we do this…

Eleanor finished for her.

"Calloway will do anything to stop us."

Nathan took a deep breath.

— So we have to overtake him.

*****

Geneva, Switzerland.

Sir Jonathan Calloway sat at a long, dark table in his office.

Opposite him stood Alexander Wren.

Wren looked tense.

—Bishop and Price escaped.

Calloway didn't look up from his report.

- I know.

Wren frowned.

— Why are you still calm?

Calloway smiled slightly.

— Because they will do exactly what I expect.

Wren narrowed his eyes.

- What do you mean?

Calloway picked up the report and threw it on the table.

— They will try to publish the list.

Wren nodded.

— And what shall we do with it?

Calloway stood up and walked to the window, looking out at the city.

— We'll make sure no one believes them.

*****

Nathan and Rachel found themselves on a deserted road where an old jeep was waiting for them.

Eleanor opened the passenger door.

— Where to now?

Hayes looked at his laptop screen.

— I know one place. There's a journalist in Berlin we can trust.

Nathan looked at him.

— Who is that?

Hayes started the engine.

—Michael Carter.

Rachel looked at Eleanor.

— Is this the same Carter who exposed the NSA scandal?

Hayes nodded.

— Yes. If anyone can pass it on, it's him.

Nathan got into the jeep.

— That means we're going to Berlin.

*****

Berlin, Germany

Michael Carter sat at the bar of a small café in Kreuzberg, stirring his coffee with a spoon.

A woman sat down next to him. She had short blond hair and a watchful gaze.

— We got the message.

Carter looked at her.

— From whom?

The woman handed him the phone.

There was an email on the screen.

"I have information that could bring down the entire government. Let's meet."

Signed: H. Bishop

Carter looked at the woman.

— Is it real?

She nodded.

— Yes.

Carter smiled slightly.

— So let's see what they have to say.

*****

Nathan and Rachel were on a plane flying to Berlin.

Rachel looked at Nathan.

— Do you think Carter is a good choice?

Nathan looked at her.

— We have no other.

Hayes spoke quietly:

— If we reveal this, Concordia will be finished.

Eleanor looked out the window.

— What if we don't succeed?

Nathan looked at her seriously.

— It won't matter anymore.

Rachel tightened her fingers on the arm of the chair.

— Because we'll be dead.

*****

Geneva.

Calloway looked at Wren.

—Bishop and Price are on their way to Berlin.

Wren nodded.

— Do you want me to stop them?

Calloway smiled slightly.

- NO.

Wren frowned.

- Why?

Calloway raised his glass of wine.

— Because when they get there, the whole world will be convinced that they are traitors.

Wren looked at him carefully.

— How will you do it?

Calloway set his glass down and reached for the phone.

— All we have to do is reveal our first version.

He pressed the button.

And at that point, headlines started appearing on CNN, BBC and Reuters.

"Nathan Bishop and Rachel Price Wanted for Treason."

"Terrorist network shattered – former lawyers at the head of international conspiracy."

"Bishop and Price – the most wanted men in the world."

Calloway smiled slightly.

— Now they can publish whatever they want.

"Nobody will believe them anyway."

*****

The plane landed at Berlin airport at 3:47 a.m.

Nathan, Rachel, Eleanor, and Hayes walked through the terminal, keeping their faces in the shadows, hiding their faces under hoods.

Every screen in the departures hall displayed the same headlines:

"Nathan Bishop and Rachel Price – The Most Wanted People in the World"

"Treason! Former lawyers implicated in international conspiracy"

"Have terrorists infiltrated the power structures?"

Rachel looked at Nathan.

— We are dead.

Nathan clenched his jaw.

— Not until the world knows the truth.

Eleanor looked at Hayes.

— Carter is waiting?

Hayes nodded.

— Yes. But he said we have to be careful. They're already tracking his movements.

Rachel looked around the airport.

— How long do we have before someone recognizes us?

Hayes glanced at his watch.

— Maybe ten minutes.

Nathan looked at Rachel.

— We're leaving through the back door. Find us transport.

Rachel nodded and started calling her contacts.

Eleanor looked at Nathan.

— If Concordia controls the media, we're already doomed.

Nathan looked her straight in the eyes.

— So we have to destroy their system from the inside.

*****

Michael Carter waited in his rented apartment in west Berlin, looking at his whiteboard full of photos and notes.

He had before him the articles on Concordia, the names of Royce, Wren, and Calloway.

He had known for years that there was some invisible structure that ruled the world.

Now he finally had a chance to prove it.

He reached for the phone and called his contact in the German government.

— I need security.

He heard an impatient voice on the other end.

" Carter, if you really have them on your property, you're done for."

Carter smiled slightly.

— We'll see.

He hung up and looked at the door.

Just a few more minutes.

The Jeep stopped in front of the apartment building.

Nathan looked at Rachel.

— Ready?

Rachel nodded.

— Let's do it.

Eleanor and Hayes got out first, checking the area.

Hayes looked at the laptop.

— I don't see any active tracking signals.

Nathan looked at the building.

— That means they're already inside.

Rachel pulled out her gun.

— So why are we still here?

Nathan smiled slightly.

— Because we have no choice.

They moved toward the door.

Carter was already waiting for them.

Carter opened the door and looked at them tensely.

— Quickly. We don't have much time.

They went inside and closed the door behind them.

Rachel looked at him sharply.

— Can we trust you?

Carter shrugged.

— If they kill me along with you, then that means yes.

Hayes connected the laptop to his system.

— We need to get this out to the media.

Carter looked at the screen.

— List?

Nathan nodded.

—Names . Bank accounts. Evidence that Concordia controls governments around the world.

Carter narrowed his eyes.

— If true, it's the biggest leak in history.

Rachel looked at him.

— So we publish.

Carter took a deep breath and leaned over the keyboard.

— Give me five minutes.

*****

Geneva.

Calloway sat in his office, staring at the screen.

One of his technicians looked at him worriedly.

— Sir, we have a problem.

Calloway turned around slowly.

- What's going on?

The man swallowed.

— Someone is trying to send the list to international news outlets right now.

Calloway smiled slightly.

- Where?

— Berlin.

Calloway looked at Wren.

— So it's Carter.

Wren nodded.

— What are we doing?

Calloway picked up the phone.

— We're locking them up.

*****

Hayes looked at the screen.

— We are sending…

Everyone held their breath.

Files started loading onto the servers.

Rachel looked at Nathan.

— Is this what's happening?

Nathan nodded.

— If this succeeds, the whole world will know the truth.

Eleanor looked at Carter.

— How long will this take?

Carter looked at the screen.

— Just one more minute.

And then the lights in the apartment went out.

Hayes looked at the screen.

— We lost the signal.

Rachel glanced at the door.

— There's someone here.

At that same moment the door exploded.

Nathan and Rachel fell to the floor, shielding themselves from shards of wood and glass.

Carter dropped to the ground, holding the laptop.

Armed men in black uniforms ran inside .

Eleanor opened fire first, hitting one of the attackers.

Rachel turned to Nathan.

— We have to protect the laptop!

Nathan grabbed the computer and threw it to Hayes.

— Secure your files!

Hayes threw himself behind the couch, trying to regain the signal.

Carter shouted:

— It's the CIA!

Nathan looked at Rachel.

— No. It's Concordia.

Rachel looked at Eleanor.

— We have to get out of here!

Nathan looked at Carter.

— Do you know an escape route?

Carter nodded.

— Yes. But we have to get through them.

Nathan smiled slightly.

— So let the fight begin.

Shots echoed in the cramped room.

Rachel threw herself backward, dodging the volley of bullets.

Nathan covered Hayes as he tried to complete the file transfer.

Carter yelled:

— We have to hurry!

Eleanor shot at the nearest attacker and looked at Rachel.

— If we stay, we will die!

Nathan looked at Hayes.

— How much longer?!

Hayes shouted:

— Thirty seconds!

Rachel looked at Nathan.

— We don't have thirty seconds.

Nathan looked at Carter.

— Find us a way out. Now.

*****

Gunshots still echoed through the apartment, and the air was full of smoke and dust.

Nathan covered Hayes as he desperately tried to regain contact.

Rachel threw herself behind an overturned table and fired several rounds at the attackers.

Eleanor screamed:

— We have to move!

Carter typed something on his phone, then looked at them.

— There's a back exit! But it's a dead end now!

Nathan looked at Hayes.

— How much time?

Hayes slammed his fist on the keyboard.

— Signal returned! Transmitting!

Everyone held their breath.

A loading bar appeared on the screen.

87%... 90%... 95%...

Rachel looked at Nathan.

— It's happening.

And then a stun grenade flew through the broken window.

Nathan lunged at Rachel, knocking her to the ground just before the explosion.

Blinding light and deafening sound filled the room.

Hayes screamed and covered his ears, and Carter fell to the ground, grabbing his laptop.

Eleanor tried to raise the gun, but before she could pull the trigger, someone kicked her in the chest, throwing her against the wall.

New attackers entered the room .

Rachel blinked, trying to regain her bearings, and saw two men in black uniforms lift Nathan and pin him against the wall.

Hayes shouted:

— Files uploaded!

Nathan looked at the laptop screen.

100%

Rachel rose to her knees and looked at Eleanor.

But Eleanor was unconscious.

One of the attackers approached her and checked her pulse.

Then he looked at his superior.

— She's dead.

Rachel felt something inside her break.

Nathan looked at Eleanor's body and felt anger rising within him.

Rachel clenched her fists, trying to hold back tears.

Carter raised his hands as if trying to surrender.

One of the attackers looked at him.

— Where are the files?

Carter did not respond.

The second guard walked up and hit him in the face with the butt of his rifle.

Carter fell to the floor.

Nathan took a step forward, but the attacker pressed the barrel of the gun to his temple.

— You move and I'll shoot.

Rachel looked at Nathan, then at Hayes, who was still holding the laptop.

One of the attackers looked at the screen.

— Files gone.

The group leader cursed under his breath.

— We're taking them.

*****

The car raced through the deserted streets of Berlin.

Rachel sat in the backseat, tied up with plastic ties.

Nathan was next to her, with a split lip and a bruise on his cheek.

Hayes sat in the front, his eyes full of panic.

Carter was silent.

One of the attackers, sitting across from Nathan, looked at them mockingly.

— Did you think you could defeat us?

Rachel looked at him coldly.

— No. We thought we could tell the truth.

The attacker laughed.

— And who will believe you?

The car turned onto a side street and stopped in front of a warehouse on the outskirts of town.

The doors opened and everyone was brutally dragged outside.

Nathan looked around.

This was the place of execution.

Nathan, Rachel, Hayes, and Carter were thrown to the ground.

The group leader took out his gun and looked at them.

— It's over.

Nathan looked at Rachel.

— If I had to choose, I wouldn't want to die in Berlin.

Rachel smiled slightly, despite the pain.

— Me neither.

The commander raised his weapon.

— Do you have any last words?

Nathan looked him straight in the eye.

— Yes.

The commander raised an eyebrow.

- I'm listening.

Nathan smiled.

— We are not alone.

And then the warehouse lights exploded and a burst of gunfire echoed through the darkness.

Bullets tore through the air.

Rachel threw herself to the ground, trying to avoid the fire.

Nathan rolled onto his side and kicked his attacker in the knee, sending him to the ground.

Masked people emerged from the darkness.

Their weapons were precise and their shots were deadly.

Rachel looked at one of them and froze.

It was Eleanor.

Alive.

Eleanor looked at her and winked.

— Did you miss me?

Nathan raised his eyebrows.

— We thought you were dead.

Eleanor smiled slightly.

— It's the best cover.

Rachel looked at her.

— Who are they?

Eleanor looked at her people.

— Allies.

Nathan looked at the fallen attackers.

— So we have a chance?

Eleanor handed him the gun.

— If you still want to finish what you started.

Nathan looked at Rachel.

— We're going for Calloway.

Rachel smiled.

— Let's do it.

*****

Geneva.

Calloway stood in his office, staring at the television screen.

Concordia's list has been published.

But instead of chaos and revolution…

The world was silent.

Calloway smiled slightly.

Wren looked at him.

— People don't react.

Calloway sighed.

— Because they don't want to know.

Wren frowned.

— So what now?

Calloway looked out the window.

— We kill them all.

*****

Nathan, Rachel, Eleanor, Hayes, and Carter sat in their hidden hiding place, staring at the laptop screen.

Concordia's list was everywhere.

The New York Times, the Guardian, Le Monde, Al Jazeera – all the major media outlets had access to the files.

But there was still silence on TV .

Rachel clenched her fists.

— Why is no one talking about this?

Hayes shook his head.

— Concordia anticipated this move.

Nathan looked at him.

- What do you mean?

Hayes pointed at the screen.

— Before we published the list, they had already questioned its authenticity. Now all the media are saying it's Russian disinformation.

Rachel looked at Nathan.

— So we lost?

Nathan closed his eyes for a second, then looked at Eleanor.

— No. Not yet.

Carter leaned against the wall.

— Concordia will win unless we find a way to make people believe it.

Eleanor looked at Nathan.

— So what do we do?

Nathan looked up.

— We have to find Calloway.

Rachel raised an eyebrow.

— To kill him?

Nathan shook his head.

— No. To force him to confess.

Geneva, Switzerland.

Sir Jonathan Calloway stood on the terrace of his mansion, sipping whiskey and looking out at the lights of the city.

Wren stood next to him, holding the phone.

—Bishop and Price are still alive.

Calloway smiled slightly.

— Still like this.

Wren narrowed his eyes.

— What if they really find me?

Calloway looked at him calmly.

— They won't find it.

Wren sighed.

— And what if?

Calloway smiled slightly.

— That means I want them to find me.

*****

Nathan and Rachel sat in a small van parked on the outskirts of Geneva.

Eleanor checked the weapons while Hayes worked on intercepting the satellite signals.

Carter looked at Nathan.

" How do you plan to get Calloway to confess?"

Nathan looked at him coldly.

— People like him aren't afraid of death. They're afraid of shame.

Rachel narrowed her eyes.

— So you want to force him to talk live?

Nathan nodded.

— We need to get his words online before he can stop it.

Hayes looked at the screen.

— I have something.

Nathan and Rachel stepped closer.

" Calloway is having a private meeting in Geneva tonight. At the Royal Savoy Hotel."

Eleanor looked at Nathan.

— So we have it.

Nathan took a deep breath.

— Yes. But that means this is our last chance.

Rachel looked at him seriously.

— So let's do it.

*****

Hotel Royal Savoy, Geneva.

The luxurious penthouse apartment was full of influential people.

Politicians, generals, bank presidents.

Sir Jonathan Calloway sat at the table, listening to reports from his advisors.

Wren leaned toward him.

—Bishop and Price are in town.

Calloway didn't look surprised.

— Of course they are.

Wren looked at him carefully.

— You're not going to evacuate?

Calloway smiled slightly.

— No. I'm waiting for them.

*****

Nathan, Rachel, Eleanor, and Hayes slipped through the back of the hotel using fake IDs.

Carter was waiting outside in the van, ready to take over the live broadcast.

Nathan looked at Rachel.

— Are you ready?

Rachel smiled slightly.

— No. But that's nothing new.

They entered the elevator and pressed the button for the top floor.

Eleanor checked the gun.

— If something goes wrong, we're not getting out of here alive.

Nathan looked at her.

— So we can't make a mistake.

The elevator stopped.

The door opened onto a luxury apartment.

And then all the lights in the hotel went out.

For a few seconds there was complete silence.

Then there were screams.

Guests at Calloway's meeting began to panic as the security system went down.

Rachel looked at Nathan.

— Is that Hayes?

Hayes spoke over the radio:

— Yes. You have five minutes before they reset the system.

Nathan looked at Eleanor.

— Find Calloway.

Rachel moved first, pushing her way through the crowd.

Nathan walked close behind her, his hand resting on the gun.

And then they saw him.

Sir Jonathan Calloway stood at the back of the room, calm, impassive, waiting.

Nathan looked at Rachel.

— He knew we would be here.

Calloway smiled slightly.

— Of course I knew.

Calloway looked at Nathan and Rachel as if their presence amused him.

— I wanted you to come here.

Nathan raised his gun.

- Why?

Calloway smiled.

— Because I want you to see how you lose.

Rachel narrowed her eyes.

— Do you think this is over?

Calloway looked at her calmly.

— Yes. Because you've already lost.

Nathan looked at Hayes over the radio.

— Are we broadcasting?

Hayes spoke on the phone:

— Yes. Live.

Nathan smiled slightly.

" So say it again, Calloway. Tell the whole world you own them."

Calloway looked at them.

And then he realized it was a trap.

Calloway looked at Nathan and Rachel, then slowly began to smile.

— Clever.

Nathan gripped the gun tighter.

"The whole world can hear you, Calloway.

Calloway turned to the crowd of politicians, generals and bank presidents who stared at him in shock.

—So the whole world just found out I'm the biggest threat?

Rachel took a step forward.

— Yes.

Calloway looked at her without a trace of fear.

— No. The whole world just found out that you are the biggest threat.

And then the televisions in the hall turned on.

A live broadcast of CNN appeared on every screen.

The presenter spoke in a calm, cool tone:

"Confirmed: Nathan Bishop and Rachel Price, leaders of an international terrorist network, have been located in Geneva. Swiss intelligence services are on their way."

"A leaked list that purported to reveal secret Concordia organization has been denied by the CIA as part of a Russian disinformation operation."

Rachel felt a cold chill run down her spine.

Nathan stared at the screens, unable to believe what he was seeing.

Calloway laughed quietly.

— You never had a chance.

Rachel looked at Hayes, who was whispering into the phone:

— They hijacked the transmission.

Nathan stepped forward, aiming the gun at Calloway.

— It's over.

Calloway raised an eyebrow.

- Really?

He waved his hand at the security guards.

Nobody moved.

Nathan frowned.

Calloway smiled slightly.

— These people are too high up to risk having their names appear on subsequent lists.

Nathan looked at the gathered businessmen and politicians.

Everyone looked at him in horror.

Not because Calloway was telling the truth.

But because he was still in control of everything.

Eleanor suddenly said over the radio:

— You have 60 seconds before they come in here.

Rachel looked at Calloway.

— This is not the end.

Calloway's smile widened.

—Of course not. Because you never had control.

Nathan looked at Rachel.

— We have to get out.

Rachel didn't want to leave.

But she knew they had no choice.

Calloway raised his glass of whiskey.

— Thank you. The world will need me even more now.

Nathan looked him straight in the eye.

— It's not over yet.

And then they threw a smoke grenade and ran away.

They ran through the hotel corridors, their footsteps echoing.

Hayes spoke over the radio:

— You have an exit on the roof.

Eleanor was already ready at the helicopter.

— Move!

Rachel looked at Nathan.

— We lost it, didn't we?

Nathan did not respond.

But she knew it was.

They ran to the roof and jumped into the helicopter.

Eleanor lifted the machine off the ground.

Below, you could see the services entering the hotel.

Calloway didn't even move.

Rachel felt for the first time in her life that they had truly lost.

*****

The helicopter was flying over the Alps when Eleanor looked at Nathan.

— What now?

Nathan looked at the clouds.

- I don't know.

Rachel closed her eyes.

— The world did not believe it.

Hayes shook his head.

— It's not that they didn't believe. They just... didn't want to.

Nathan was right.

Calloway didn't win because he had power.

He won because people preferred to believe a lie.

Rachel looked at Nathan.

— Is it over?

Nathan finally looked at her.

— No. But this is not our fight anymore.

*****

A year later

Rachel sat on a terrace in a small South American village, sipping coffee.

Nathan sat down next to her.

- The news?

Rachel handed him the phone.

The headline said:

"Sir Jonathan Calloway elected as UN special adviser."

Nathan was not surprised.

Rachel looked at him.

— And what now?

Nathan smiled slightly.

— Now we wait.

Rachel narrowed her eyes.

— For what?

Nathan put down the newspaper.

— For the day when the world is finally ready for the truth.

*****

Geneva, Switzerland.

Calloway stood atop a skyscraper, looking out over the city.

Behind him stood Alexander Wren.

Wren looked at him.

— Do you think they will come back?

Calloway smiled slightly.

— No. They're done.

Wren glanced at his watch.

— And if not?

Calloway turned and looked him straight in the eye.

— We'll find them first...

Made in the USA
Las Vegas, NV
06 February 2025

17675107R00125